# DARK FUTURES

## RUSS CROSSLEY
## RITA SCHULZ

53RD STREET PUBLISHING

# DARK FUTURES

A Collection By

Russ Crossley and Rita Schulz

Published by 53rd Street Publishing
Offices in Gibsons, B.C. Canada and Lincoln City Oregon,
U.S.A

Dark Futures

Cover art ©grandfailure/depositphotos
Cover designed by R. Edgewood
Cover design and layout © 2020 by 53rd Street Publishing
Print ISBN 978-1-927621-74-5

53rd Street Publishing
Head office: Gibsons B.C. Canada
www.53rdstreetpublishing.com

# ACKNOWLEDGMENTS

Thank you to all our friends and loved ones for their support during these challenging times.

# DEDICATION

*For our parents. Thank you.*

# INTRODUCTION

I write this in the midst of the worst pandemic to strike this world in over a hundred years. This collection is a group of stories designed to explore possible world ending futures. These were written a few years before the events we are living through now as warnings of what might be. Read them, learn from them, and hopefully together we will survive these uncertain times and those they may lay ahead.

Stay safe and be well.

R. Edgewood

Gibsons, B.C.

April 2020

# SCAVENGERS

Russ Crossley

Tey Wilks stole a peek over the jagged rocks of the sun-dried, moss-covered, partially collapsed stone wall overlooking the vast rows of shabby one-hundred-and-sixty-story buildings running as far as the horizon from the hill he was on. The odors of rotting garbage, mold, and stale food wafted over him carried by the constant breeze, but didn't penetrate his consciousness. He had grown up around the cesspools of this city of over five hundred million residents so his senses were numb to such an odiferous atmosphere. In all his long life, he had never once been outside city limits so the massive city was all he knew. He swept the strands of his shoulder-length chestnut-brown hair away from his face.

He then dropped back down behind the wall, fearful a marauder gang might spot him. Marauder gangs conducted sweeps, looking for citizens weakened by hunger and unable to defend themselves, or the injured, or those suffering from disease.

The government paid the gangs a bounty for each citizen

they captured, but there were rumors the gangs would take any citizen they caught outside their homes after twilight.

Since the atmosphere had grown thick with pollutants, twilight was now a moveable target depending on the weather. If it rained heavily enough to knock down the pollutants in the air, twilight could be delayed. Of course, given the infrequency of rainfall, twilight conditions had grown longer and longer in recent years. Soon the smog would be so thick twilight would own the daylight hours. Consequently, with each passing year the marauder gangs had become bolder.

The rumors said those citizens weakened from hunger and those suffering debilitating injuries were executed at government facilities. The rumors also said a team of immunologists assessed the diseased. Citizens with a communicable disease were isolated for experimental purposes.

This is where the substantiated rumors stopped. No one knew what these experiments were meant to determine, or what happened to the citizens after the experiments were complete. This is where the wild speculation and conspiracy theories sprouted like mushrooms in a damp basement.

Tey's favorite of these crazy theories said once diseases were isolated, they were tested on cities and millions died in agony. But since communication between cities was spotty, this had never been confirmed. No one he knew, or ever heard of, had died from illness or natural causes in over a hundred years. The government wasn't about to reveal what they were doing to the citizenry. They controlled every aspect of life on the planet.

Moving away from the wall, crouching low to shield himself from anyone looking in his direction, he quickly came to the end of the sun-browned grassy area behind the wall. Tey's mission was to scavenge for food, bottles of fresh water, and other supplies needed by his pod of apartments.

A pod consisted of six apartments occupied by one hundred and forty-eight people. He was one of sixteen volunteer scavengers from his pod, scouring the city for the ever more precious supplies. Competing scavengers were as big a threat as the marauders, hence Tey was armed with two pistols and four knives of varying lengths, hidden about his ragged, soiled clothes. He would kill if necessary.

His survival and that of his pod depended on acquiring the necessary quota of supplies. No one was about to stand in his way and live if they tried to prevent him from reaching his quota, as far as he was concerned. If he failed to meet his quota too often, his pod mates would break his legs and leave him outside for the next marauder sweep. He'd seen it done many times in his seventy-two years.

He froze, sucking in his breath, and his heart began to beat rapidly when something to his right made a cracking sound. He hoped it was a competitor and not a marauder gang. Peering into the growing darkness, he was a little relieved to see a single figure shrouded in shadow move near the deserted warehouse across the field from him. He would have stood very little chance of surviving if this had been a marauder gang.

Swallowing hard, he scurried to his right hoping to flank the potential threat. Muffled footsteps came from somewhere to his left.

Tey fell on his belly in the dry grass and pulled one of his pistols from its holster. He held it out, aiming into the darkness. His own rapid breathing echoed in his head.

There was a flash suppressor affixed to the barrel of his gun, so even if he missed, the target wouldn't be able to see where the shot came from. His eyes had adjusted to the darkness so he could see a human-shaped silhouette standing near the opening where the door used to be to enter the warehouse.

After taking careful aim, he shouted for the person to freeze and drop their weapon. The shadow dropped to the ground and a burst of gunfire, accompanied by brilliant muzzle flashes, sent a barrage of bullets whizzing over his head. Tey fired back, three successive shots aimed at the source of the flashes followed by a satisfying cry of pain, then stillness.

Tey waited, straining to hear any sounds from the target. After several minutes the tension in his body eased and he stood and began to move toward the warehouse, keeping his gun at the ready just in case. Finally he stood over the body and realized his shots had been more accurate than he'd hoped. The woman, dressed in a head-to-toe one-piece black jumpsuit, lay on her back, her dead gaze staring up at him. Holstering his own gun, he knelt beside her and quickly found her gun and two knives, which he stuffed into his belt. It didn't appear she'd managed to scavenge any supplies, which was too bad. It would have made his job easier to steal what he needed from a corpse, at least for today.

Realizing the brief firefight would attract unwanted attention, he hurried away until he was once again swallowed by the darkness. Soon he was following an old dirt road into an area of the city he had never been in before. He'd been tracking a government caravan for several days, hoping the vehicles had plenty of food and other supplies he could poach from without being noticed. The tracks of the convoy of trucks left deep ruts in the roads so they were carrying something heavy. Very heavy given the depth of the tire tracks.

That woman he just killed must have been on the same mission as him, which meant there were probably other scavengers around. He had to be careful.

As he walked over a slight rise in the road, he saw lights coming from a massive warehouse about a mile away. He estimated the building was several acres in size and could easily swallow a fleet of trucks. Scanning the terrain visible between him and the warehouse, he couldn't make out a lot of details in this darkness, but what he could make out caused him concern. There wasn't a lot of cover to hide his approach.

A marauder gang, or the security force no doubt guarding

the convoy, would take him out long before he reached the objective.

Considering his options for several seconds, he decided to try the direct approach and see how good the security truly was. He walked in the middle of the road until he came to a wire fence. Along the top of the fence were closed-circuit cameras that swiveled to cover the length of the fencing, both east and west of the gate. The heavy steel padlock affixed to the gate prevented him from easy access. But there were no guards, armed or otherwise, standing at or near the entrance to the warehouse. The doors were closed so he couldn't see the interior, but a row of small windows ran the length of the building approximately five feet from the roofline. Golden rays of light were visible through the windows. They appeared to fluctuate rather than provide steady illumination. He wondered what that meant.

The smell of mud and grass permeated Tey's senses...and it suddenly dawned on him the grass didn't smell sunburned as it did everywhere else in the city. How was this possible? His eyes narrowed as he studied the warehouse and the surrounding area in front of the warehouse doors. There was something odd about this building. But what?

His eyes went wide. It isn't old.

The fence, the cameras, the warehouse itself were all newer than anything he had ever seen. As the population density increased dramatically beginning seventy years ago, all construction stopped when all available building sites were occupied. Almost every continent contained massive cities with multibillions of citizens. One world government maintained strict control of food and water supplies and other daily necessities after the worldwide financial system collapsed decades ago.

"Don't move," said a stern male voice behind him. Tey froze

where he stood and closed his eyes, expecting to be shot at any second. "Check him," said the voice.

A rough pair of hands pushed Tey face-first into the fence and began to search him. Soon his guns and knives, and those he'd stolen off the dead scavenger, were on the ground around him. "Okay, step back. No sudden moves." Tey did as instructed and waited as two hushed voices, one male, the other female, discussed in rapid-fire tones something for a minute or two. Finally the female voice instructed him to turn around.

When Tey did he found himself facing two scavengers he knew. Malt and Ergo from zone 5567.2. The three of them had cooperated on a successful mission a few years back. Between them they split a massive haul that provided supplies for their respective apartments for five weeks.

"You two interested in a pact?" Tey said.

Malt and Ergo exchanged looks, distain in their hazel eyes. The shorter, pale blonde Ergo pulled her pistol from her holster. "Hold on." Tey raised his hands. "Listen, I've been following this convoy for weeks and it is the largest concentration of supplies I have ever seen. Far larger than the last time we worked together."

Ergo briefly shifted her gaze to Malt. "Some of the food we stole last time was rotten within a week. Ours caused the loss of two babies," Malt growled, running a thick hand through his thin gray hair. The jagged scar running down his left cheek paled as he spoke.

"I'm very sorry, but there was no way to know. Some of our food was spoiled too." He nodded toward the warehouse. "This warehouse is newly constructed. Something strange is going on here. Something we should all profit from."

"Why should we trust you?" Ergo spat the words. She took a step closer to Tey, raising the gun to waist height as she did so.

"I witnessed soldiers loading boxes in the back of one of the trucks at one of their stops."

Malt arched an eyebrow at him. "So what?"

"I'll kill 'im," said Ergo, a slow grin spreading across her lips as her humorless eyes narrowed. "And I'll enjoy it."

"The boxes were labeled emergency supplies."

Malt froze and his eyes widened. "Hold on, Ergo. He may be on to something."

Ergo scowled at her partner. She obviously really wanted to kill Tey. With a grunt of distain, she holstered her weapon and stepped back beside her partner. She crossed her arms over her chest and scowled at Tey.

"What do you think was in those boxes?" asked Malt.

Tey shrugged. "I don't know exactly, but when they had the back of the truck open for loading, it was packed top to bottom with boxes. And the convoy was at least fifty trucks." A sardonic smile spread across Tey's square-jawed features. "That's a lot of emergency supplies."

"Why do we need you?" asked Ergo sarcastically.

"Because I'm stupid enough to be the bait to get us inside." He nodded toward the warehouse behind them.

Malt grinned and nodded. He understood.

---

Tey glanced over his left shoulder and peered into the darkness. He knew Malt and Ergo were close by but he couldn't see them. They had managed to sneak up on him undetected so it wasn't surprising they were invisible to what he was about to do. It did feel good he had his weapons hidden on his body again, but it was unlikely he'd get to use them as he wanted to.

Swallowing hard, he approached the massive padlock. He pulled out a pistol and fired a single shot at the lock. The bullet made a sharp ping as it ricocheted off the heavy gauge steel without breaking the lock. An earsplitting siren erupted with three short blasts in the quiet, startling him, then went silent once again.

He put away his pistol and waited with his arms hanging loose at his sides. No sense in drawing unnecessary fire.

Three heavily armed soldiers appeared through the warehouse door. They wore head-to-toe body armor, including Kevlar helmets, and hefted large caliber automatic rifles.

"Freeze," one of them shouted at him. The three soldiers fanned out, two acting as guards training their weapons to the left and right of the solider who had shouted at Tey and was now pointing his weapon at him. Tey could imagine what would have happened if he'd actually destroyed the lock, however unlikely. I would have extra holes in my body.

"Hands up," instructed the solider aiming his weapon at him. Tey did as he was told, keeping his eyes on the solider doing the talking.

"Any sign of others?" The two guards shouted the all clear but kept their weapons at the ready. "Mills, pop the lock." The large man to the left of the guy Tey assumed was the leader slung his weapon around his body and pulled out a small black device from his pocket. He pressed a button on the device and the padlock disengaged. "Open the gate."

Mills removed the padlock and swung the gate inward while the other guard remained a few paces away, continuing to scan the area with the weapon.

Once outside they surrounded Tey and the one in command stepped close. "Name?"

"Tey Wilks, sir."

"You military?" Tey shook his head. "Then don't call me sir. My name is Ruse. I'm in command. And you, buddy, are an intruder on government property."

"I'm with a marauder gang," explained Tey.

Ruse lifted the goggles covering his eyes and arched at eyebrow at Tey, then looked him up and down. "Is that so?" He thought about Tey's explanation for several seconds before continuing. "Why are you alone? Marauders always operate in gangs."

Tey nodded. "My gang was ambushed by a group of scavengers...I was the only survivor. I've come here to get help. They could be close by."

Tey watched the three soldiers tense, just as he'd hoped. Two of them started to walk away from the gate, also just as he'd hoped, their backs to him and Ruse. Suddenly there were two soft thumps and the two soldiers dropped to the ground. Ruse began pulling his side arm from the holster on his belt, but Tey stepped forward before Ruse had it fully out of the holster and punched the man in the center of his chest as hard as he could. Ruse was still off balance so he fell backward, landing hard on his back. A third thump and Ruse slumped back and lay still. Tey saw a dart sticking from the man's arm.

"Hey, why didn't you just shoot these guys?" Tey said to Malt when he appeared from the darkness.

"The military gets very pissed with scavengers who kill soldiers and we don't need the heat." Malt kicked at one of Ruse's boots to make sure he wasn't playing possum. When Ruse didn't move, Malt grunted. "Fast acting," he added, anticipating Tey's next question. "They'll be out for hours. Provided the warehouse isn't littered with these types, we should have plenty of time to pick over the contents of those boxes." He glanced at Ergo, who had joined them from where she'd been hiding.

"I know how to hotwire their trucks," Tey offered, hoping it was enough not to get shot now that they were inside. They needed to see that his continued living had some benefit for them, especially as they felt the rotten supplies from their last joint venture were his fault.

Ergo frowned. "What kind of trucks are they?"

"Army issue. Probably those Mack models they favor.

Usually a hybrid engine these days. I figure it burns used cooking oils and electric." Tey watched Ergo's uncertain gaze shift to Malt, who cursed under his breath. She was the hotwire expert, but she'd never hotwired military vehicles. They'd need these trucks to move this quantity of supplies. Tey had just had his survival card punched, at least until the trucks were ready to roll. He needed to negotiate the rest of the way.

"Listen, Malt, I'd be willing to split half of my share between you two if my safety is assured."

Malt's eyes shifted briefly to his partner. Her mouth had become a thin line. She didn't want to make the deal. She was eager to kill him. A little too eager from Tey's perspective.

Malt shook his head and grinned at Tey. "Good play." He shrugged. "Sure, why not. Besides, we can use the help loading the stuff." He eyed Ergo. "Stand down. Three pairs of hands make the work go quickly and the haul larger."

Ergo avoided his gaze. "Yeah. Okay," she whispered gruffly before she swung her rifle, attached to a sling, behind her back.

"Let's adjourn this for now and see what if anything we discover in the warehouse," Malt said, nodding toward the massive structure behind them. They nodded in unison.

Once inside with their pistols out ready for any opposition, they discovered rows upon rows of steel shelving stacked high with boxes, the words EMERGENCY SUPPLIES emblazoned across them, running down the right side of the massive facility as far as they were able to see. On the left side of the warehouse was parked a fleet of military trucks identical to the ones he'd seen loading when he first started on this journey.

Tey's heart nearly leapt out of his chest with excitement at the sight. There was no way he'd had any idea the potential haul would be this big. If he'd known, he would have brought the entire scavenger team from his pod with him. Even then they would only have made a dent in a load this big, which was a double-edged sword in the scavenger game.

Hauling away all they could carry would hopefully not attract too much attention. The military expected some leakage, as they called it. Small losses were tolerated, large ones were unforgiveable and forced serious retribution with heavy weapons. No pod would ever permit their scavengers to attract such attention if they wanted to remain among the living. Though at times Tey wouldn't call their day-to-day survival living.

Malt ran up to one of the shelving units and began to open one of the boxes. Ergo joined him and together they dragged the box from the shelf onto the warehouse floor. The echo of their footsteps and their excited but hushed tones echoed off the faraway walls and the vastness of this place. Tey sniffed the air and was assaulted by a strong odor of machine oil. Something seemed wrong, but he couldn't quite tell what. It was as if there was a word just on the tip of his tongue he couldn't remember.

Malt froze when the box was open. He stared inside, wide-eyed as if stunned by his discovery. Ergo cursed under her breath. Tey joined them and immediately saw what had caused such reactions after the initial excitement.

The box was filled with glass jars much like the old canning jars he'd pilfered in his early days of scavenging. Inside the jars were sealed glass tubes filled with purplish liquid.

"What the hell is this?" said Malt, rising to his feet, his features twisted in rage. He glared at Tey, his hands curled into fists.

Suddenly the sounds of leather boots running and the click of safeties being disengaged filled the vast warehouse. "Don't move," said a deep male voice behind them.

A sharp, sudden pain struck the middle of his back. It made him start with surprise and he sucked a breath in. Quickly his mind whirled and darkness closed in until the world disappeared into blackness.

"End program."

The scene of the warehouse disappeared and with it the soldiers and the scavengers Malt, Ergo, and Tey. All that remained was an empty chamber with reflective walls and a matching floor.

"So, Mr. Wilks, what is this simulation program of yours supposed to prove?" said a bald man in a dark suit, white shirt, and a red power tie. His blue eyes were focused on the slim, wiry man across the table from him with granny glasses covering his brown eyes, grasping a data pad in his hands. In contrast to the man seated at the table, he was dressed in faded corduroy pants, worn sneakers, and a brown-and-yellow checkered shirt with no tie. His mouse-brown hair was slicked back on his narrow head.

"Well, sir, we have run this simulation one hundred and forty-seven times and the most common outcome is that approximately a hundred years from now, the world will end."

The man seated at the table arched both eyebrows. "I'm not sure I understand."

"In the next hundred years, with medical advances, life extension drugs will increase life spans around the planet upwards to more than one hundred and fifty years. At the same time, climate change will force the production of GMO foods in underground facilities adapted for darker conditions with no natural sunlight. Pollution and environmental changes will scour the Earth of most animal life and vegetation. The oceans will be drained and desalinated to create drinking water for the estimated fifty billion people on the planet."

"Okay, so we survive," said the man, raising his hands palms-up above the table. "That's good news. Not the end of the world as you so dramatically put it." He rose from the chair and smoothed his expensive suit with the palms of his hands.

"But, sir, you don't understand. Once all our resources are exhausted, the world will end."

The man in the suit arched an eyebrow at Wilks and glared at him. "How?"

"The simulation we created extrapolates that the vials in those glass jars in the warehouse in this version of the program contain a toxin designed to be powerful enough to kill ninety-five percent of the human race in one day."

The man snorted derisively and shook his head as he closed the buttons on his suit jacket with his long, tapered fingers. "You think the government is going to wipe out ninety-five percent of the human race?" He grinned to himself. "Scavengers. Marauder gangs. Cities with billions of people. Tranquilizer darts. Science fiction," he muttered dismissively under his breath.

Tey Wilks shook his head, his expression grim. "No. I do not. My simulations prove the toxin will kill every human and animal on the planet. Even microscopic life will perish. My tests confirm the formulation will be slightly off, just enough to allow it to mutate and wipe out all life on Earth."

The man chuckled. "Of course." He started to walk to the exit door. "I'll take your recommendations to the National Science Council and they will take them to the President and the United Nations Security Council. I assure you this simulation will receive the highest priority it deserves." He opened the door and the last Tey saw of him was the door slamming shut behind him.

"I'm sure it will," Tey whispered in the now quiet holo lab. They were all doomed.

# ONER DAY AT A TIME

Rita Schulz

Ellen stood wearing her purple fleece night gown on her long, wide back deck facing the Inlet with a steaming cup of coffee in her hand looking out at the water.

It was such a mild morning on the Sunshine coast on this first week of January, she couldn't believe how fortunate they were this year. It seemed that they had escaped any snow at all. Only a few cold days of below freezing at night, just enough to set her spring flowering blubs was all they'd had. She looked over at the side yard at the buds on her magnolia that were swelling and the roses that she had planted last summer, they were still in bloom only four weeks ago. Then her eyes glanced at the lads, their dogs, playing tag in the back yard. One Samson, a seven-year-old golden retriever and the other a small fourteen year-old red terrier, Rusty. The heavy rains they had for the last two week had stopped so today would be a good day to stretch their legs, they all needed a walk.

She looked back out at the water, she never tired of looking at the keyhole view they had of the Georgia Straight, the stretch of water between themselves and Vancouver Island. A well-seasoned sailboat captain had told her that there were only about eight miles of water between Gibsons and the large Vancouver Island. All she knew was when she and Lee, her husband of twenty-five years had seen this little two story home with it's level entry and walk out basement they knew they had found home. There was lots of room for family and guests and the tall evergreen and arbutus trees that surrounded it made if feel cozy, their little cabin in the woods.

As she watched the water, she realized that something was wrong. In all the time they had lived here you could get to the water by walking a long set of wooden stairs.

Kelly leaned over the railing and looked at the waves between the trees on the right side of her view. The waves were coming from the west usually that meant fair weather, but something stank, really, badly. It wasn't the pulp mill, they got the odd smell from there a couple of times a year. No, this was like Oyster Bay at very low tide, mud, dead shellfish, oysters, muscles and seaweed. It made you want to heave.

She had never, ever no matter how low the tide got had seen the bottom. There was always water covering the rocks and gravel directly below them, but not this morning.

She'd left the television on when she checked the weather station and now she heard the emergency signal. At least that's what she thought it was. She called to the dogs as she went back into the house and looked at the large television in the corner of the living room between the bay window and the built in mantel over the wood-burning fireplace.

She heard Matthew her three-year-old grandson getting up and coming into the living room and gave him a quick smile. "Honey, why don't you go and find Grandpa? Tell him I want to see him right now. Hurry please," she said. She tried to emphasize the words without scaring Matthew. The boy scooted away as the announcer came on.

"A comet hit the Pacific ocean this morning. We are expecting earth quakes in the next few minutes and tidal waves to batter the Pacific Northwest this late morning, especially the area from San Francisco to Canada," said a man who could barley contain his fear.

Ellen quickly turned off the television in case Mathew heard what was happening. She looked to the telephone should she try and call Mathew's parents? She had to at least try. Then she'd make a quick call to her other son too. She picked up the cordless phone and started to dial. All she got was a busy signal even before she finished the phone number. She put it down on the kitchen counter.

Oh God, please not that. She had heard so much about tsunamis from her friends in Oregon, all she could do is repeat what they had said to her over and over again. Get to higher ground. Get to higher ground. It was litany that kept repeating in her head. Kelly felt herself start to panic and then her rational brain kicked in. You can panic later, but right now you need to act.

"Lee, I need you to come up right now! I mean right now!" she called down to the basement. She hoped he heard her, he had to come now.

They had at most five minutes to leave and get to higher ground. She checked her watch. Okay go.

Once the earthquakes started there was no telling how the road around her would hold up and they had to get out before the tidal wave.

Okay, what do you need? And I mean need? She thought the herself as she went through her list of must have things.

She ran into the guest bedroom and grabbed a large wheeled backpack. She was like a mad woman as she ran through the house opening drawers. Grabbing three of for each of them, three socks and underwear, three tee shirts, three pants, running shoes and hiking boots. She grabbed the dog bowls, their kibble, luckily they had just gotten more the other day and their treats.

They had to get out of here. Don't dawdle she thought as she ran into the living room and grabbed the photos and albums off the mantel and the antique oak mirrored hutch.

The best place would be the Safeway parking lot at the junction of Pratt and Gibsons Road. It was very high ground and she knew that this whole area was on a massive granite vein of rock that stretched for about fifty to one hundred miles all down the coast.

The dogs came bounding into the house, barking, happy to be able to play without the benefit of the dark days and heavy rains that they had been having, which was typical of a winter in Gibsons.

She ran and slammed closed the sliding glass patio door so the dogs couldn't get out.

"Lee, I need you here right now!" Kelly yelled all pretense of niceness gone. She tried to weight her odds of how many people would be trying to get to Safeway to find safety and food and water.

She heard the basement door open and Mathew's light little boy's voice chatting to his grandfather as they came up the stairs.

"What's the problem Ellen? We're coming," he said as he walked up the stairs with her budging laptop bag in his hand. He looked over the banister and saw her dragging the case with their clothes to the front door.

He took one look at her and quickly walked to her side and put an arm around her. "What is it, one of the kids?" he asked softly in her ear.

"No, worse, much worse. A comet has hit the Pacific Ocean, there's going to be tidal waves and earthquakes. There talking like the San Andrade's Fault it finally going to let loose too," said Ellen as she watched Lee's eyes got softer as she spoke so fast most people would not be able to understand her. Then he looked around the foyer and by the front door, licked his lips and nodded.

"I know. I've got my lap-top and the mini tower," he said a as he walked into their pantry, pulled out a large cloth shopping bag went down the hall and pulled down three of his favorite paintings that she had done over the years.

"We need to get to higher ground right now," they said in unison.

"They said they don't know when things are going to happen but I figure we've got five minutes. Listen carefully," she said looking at her wristwatch. "We've used three of the already.

She quickly went through the things she had packed from flashlights with extra batteries to toilet paper and everything in between. He listened as she spoke and they started to carry things to the tan colored RAV4 they would be taking with them.

"Can you think of anything else? I don't have fresh water so I used some of our buckets and a couple of pots with tap water. I'm hoping to get some more water at the grocery store," Ellen had to stop for a minute, she was breathing so hard and her mouth was so dry she was starting to get dizzy.

Lee put his arms around her and held her in his arms. "It's going to be okay. We have Vancouver Island to take the brunt off the tidal action and as for earth quakes as you told me when we bought the house the huge granite vein under us and Mt. Capstone behind us has stood for many years and will be here for a very long time to come. We'll see how the house and your Studio do," he laughed softly as he gently pushed her short dark brown hair from her face and kissed her forehead.

They looked at each other nodded and quickly pulled the

rest of the things out of the front door and into the back of the Rave.

In Ellen's head she kept on hearing, get to higher ground, get to higher ground. "We are, we are," she mumbled under her breath to herself.

Lee and Ellen picked up Mathew, strapped him into his car seat in the back seat and then Ellen armed with a pocket full of dog treats grabbed Rusty and threw him in the rear foot well with a treat then grabbed Samson and put him the back seat too.

As she was going to close the back door, Mathew started to cry and kick his feet.

"It's okay Mathew, we're going on a car ride up to Safeway, " she said as she leaned forward and pick up a toy that had fallen onto the seat, as she did Samson decided that he would squeeze past her and he started to head up the driveway.

Ellen's heart almost stopped. She knew that Samson had been really bad lately about coming when called. She could feel her stomach clench and her mind jumped to 'what might happen'.

She had to get him in the car now. They had to leave NOW! They had to get to hire ground. Above all else they had to keep Mathew safe. And that might mean leaving Samson behind. She felt her eyes swell with tears and her vision blurred. She prepared herself, she'd have to live with whatever happened.

She only had one chance before they left.

"Okay Sampson. Come." She said with authority.

Sampson walked to the top of the driveway and sniffed their hedge. She shook the dog treats. "Sampson, cookie."

The dog looked up at her and slowly wagged his tail, his tongue lolled out from the side of his mouth. Great the dog was grinning at her thinking it was a game.

She felt Rusty jump up onto the back seat of the RAV. "Sampson, car ride. Cookie."

In her heart Ellen was begging for Sampson to come. She turned her back to the dog, shook the bad of treats and gave Rusty another cookie making sure that Sampson could see what she was doing. "Please God, please," she whispered under her breath, begging for the big dog to come.

"Get in the truck Ellen. He's wondering down the street," said Lee in a resigned, but firm voice.

She knew that she could just walk up to him and get him, but he was wandering to far away now. He'd gone a block and a half and they only had a few precious moments. She couldn't risk all their lives.

She closed the rear door and quickly walked around the truck and slid into the front passenger seat. She held back the tears, she would never forgive herself for leaving Samson, her big goofy buddy. She could feel sobs fill her chest and tears fill her eyes, she looked out of the window and tried to swallow her grief.

Maybe they would find him after this was all over. He knew the area because of their walks together, and he was smart. She bet that he'd get home before they would, but her tears wouldn't stop.

"Okay let's go!" she said as she put on her seatbelt and slammed the door closed. She took a deep breath and held onto the armrest.

Lee stepped on the gas, nothing happened. Lee tried again, but the car wouldn't start. Nothing. This had never happened to her before. He looked at Ellen. She glanced at him as she opened her door and jumped out.

"It won't start. Look grab Mathew and start up Third Street I'll meet you at Safeway or along the road," said Lee as he looked at Ellen.

She almost laughed at the suggestion. Yea, she could get a short way up the hill, but not all the way to the highway, but it was a good four to five miles away. Would she get there with a small three-year-old boy in tow in the next few minutes. Not a chance.

"Come on get out. I'll get the car going," she said. She stood to the side and Lee jumped out. She slid behind the wheel, waved her remote control key, stepped on the brake firmly, and then hit the start button once it went green.

A welcoming deep rumble greeted their ears as the car sprang to life.

"Okay, let's try this again," said Ellen and she got into her seat.

She looked up and noticed that the steady traffic in front of their door had slowed and then stopped.

"Lee, let's go up Third and then swing up Robin. I have a feeling that the traffic is plugged on Ocean View. Besides we'll constantly be going up and getting higher," said Ellen as she cleared her throat.

Lee checked the radio, there was only static on all the stations twice and nothing was on any of them, he turned it off.

"Gram, breakfast?" asked Mathew who had been very quiet up to now.

"Sure how about a nice soft blueberry bar and some water?" Ellen asked as she pulled up the large bag of snacks, juice and their small amount of bottled water. She opened a bar and handed it to him.

Ellen, rolled down her window, everything was eerily quiet. No bird song, no chitterling from squirrels, no eagles cry. She looked up, no birds, the only thing moving were the trees swaying with the wind.

"We'll go as far as we can. The Safeway lot is probably full right now. Any ideas?" asked Lee as he kept the truck steadily moving.

Suddenly the truck started to sway. A huge sixty foot maple tree in front of them started to lean and then fall. The crash shook the truck luckily it fell away from the road. Lee stopped and waited. There were only a few cars before and behind them, they all stopped as well. They continued crawling forward and arrived at the corner of Overlook and Proud and turned left. They had passed by the steep switchbacks and the s-curves on Overlook now the road was straight all the way up to the main highway, where the Safeway was.

They drove up Proud slowly there were cars and trucks in the ditch, people walking up the road carrying children and belongings. They would occasionally look behind them at the water then back toward the mountain where they were heading.

They were about a mile away from the Safeway when another earthquake hit, this time the telephone poles across the street started to fall like dominoes along the road and not across it, they kept on moving. So far so good.

"I don't think that we'll have much of a problem here in Gibsons. At least not at first. The house may even be standing. It probably won't have any glass windows left, and we won't have electricity, but I'm hoping that we still have the a working septic tank, but I guess we need electricity for that, don't we?"

Lee nodded as he watched the road and the other cars around him waiting for another quake to hit them.

"I am worried about the kids, and our family and friends in Vancouver. I think some places will be fine. Don't you?"

"I know, I'm worried too. Look out the window, can you see the ocean from here? Maybe it won't be as bad as they predict. I'm worried about the ferries," said Lee letting Ellen's question hang.

Ellen craned her head toward the water. "I don't see any... oh, now I see water. It's about half way across to the Island. I can't see what's happening on the other side of the Island in the Long Beach area. I sure hope they get clear of all this. Mathew's asleep."

Lee nodded as they were buffeted again, this time harder

and the truck slid to the right. He stopped, waited, and then proceeded slowly.

"Sason. Sason, where is he?" asked a sleepy Mathew as he woke and stretched. He started to sniffle as he looked around. "I want Sason. Here Sason!"

Ellen looked at Lee and saw tears in his eyes that he brushed away with the back of his hand. She swallowed hard trying to keep herself from getting emotional. "What do I say? How do I tell him that we just left Samson?"

"No. It's like we said, Samson went for a walk, he's exploring and we hope he's at home by the time we get back."

Ellen nodded and used her fingers to the rub the tears from her eyes. She felt like such a failure. She should have done something, she should have trained the dog better. But if that dog, no, when that dog came back he would be so trained no one would recognize him. She'd make sure of it.

"Honey, Samson went exploring, remember? Hopefully he'll be finished and at home when we get there. Do you want some water now? She reached back and unscrewed the bottle. Remember only a little bit at a time."

The little boy took the bottle and she grabbed a towel and put it on his chest in case he spilt. She watched him and smiled. He was their reason to continue on. They had to protect him and make sure that he didn't just survive but that he thrived. He was the reason they had to go to higher ground, he was the reason they would be alright.

"I was thinking of somewhere else that we could go, in the same area? Ideas?"

"How about George's place. You remember the contractor that built the studio and the fences for us?"

"Yea? Oh, the empty lot or lots in his subdivision?" asked Lee. He smiled and nodded at Ellen.

"Yea. If the empty lots are full of cars, maybe we can park

on the street. At least for tonight? We're high enough now," said Ellen looking back over her shoulder.

"Okay."

"I also um... have a shovel if we need to dig a hole. It will be just like camping when the kids were little, won't it?" Ellen looked at him and grinned, she remembered how much he hated camping.

"Honey, I'm afraid that we're going to have to take this one day at a time and hope for the best."

She was concerned over a lot of things, would they have water, would they have electricity, would they have help from the mainland. How many people would likely die without their medication, could they get it? How many would be gone in the next three weeks, three months, six months or a year?

Ellen stopped the racing thoughts in her mind, she had to focus on what was happening right now and deal with the problems and solutions in front of them.

She knew there were people that lived off the grid here on the Sunshine Coast so if they had to face this crisis this was a good place to be. Only time would tell but right now she had to calm her mind about the what-ifs.

They reached the cross roads of the main highway and drove to the other side.

Ellen felt herself relax. They were well over the tsunami level now.

"Keep driving, I see that the Safeway is full, but I still see empty lots in George's subdivision. We're going to be okay, at least for today," Ellen said as she reached over and squeezed Lee's hand.

All they could do was do their best and as Lee said take it one day at a time.

# UNNATURAL IMMORTAL

Russ Crossley

In mid-August, nights in the Tall Timbers forest are muggy and stifling, the air thick as pudding. But the tranquility of this green meadow in the middle of these elegant pines and majestic oaks provided a welcome respite for Amy Selkirk, who sat almost buried in the long, wild grasses tipped yellow by the sun. Leaning back she rested her weight on her hands, relishing the peace and quiet of the dark woods surrounding her. But even the meadow's tranquility could do little to lessen the oppressive humidity of the summer and the danger that lurked around every tree.

She was bathing in this fleeting escape from the real world.

Amy lolled her head back with her eyes closed, dreaming of her revenge while the sweet odor of wildflowers filled her nostrils, the fragrant jasmine and lavender providing a pleasant distraction. In reality, she was unable to fully relish the peace this place of retreat promised for very long.

The unquenchable thirst gripping Amy's every waking hour was like a massive weight pressing on her by some unseen force. Too often these days the hunger for blood pushed away all other thoughts. Each passing day this need became more intense, threatening to consume her. Soon Amy's humanity would disappear, completely lost in a swirling vortex of lust and death that had become her new reality.

Time was growing short.

Her sire, Argos, the vampire who made her one of the undead, had preyed on her weaknesses and insecurity, using them as weapons to take control of her and her sister by offering her immortality. She agreed to become a vampire before she realized her romantic notions of immortality were false, the truth far more terrible than she imagined and far from romantic. Argos tricked her into this existence of living death.

Early on after her transformation, she struggled with her decision to challenge her sire until she came to realize Argos was a power-mad despot bent on building his own personal empire on the bloody, broken bodies of human cattle—the ultimate goal being his quest for absolute power. He had to be stopped before he enslaved the world to his will, and Amy was determined to destroy Argos before it was too late.

Sighing, she opened her eyes and turned her head slightly to look at the corpse, her prey, in the inky blackness of the night lying facedown buried in the grass next to her.

Amy had laid him next to her after carrying him across her shoulders up the hill to this meadow. His name was Edward Lamp; he had been a plantation owner from the nearby town of Andersonville.

The late Mr. Lamp bought his cotton from slave owners, men who exploited what she still thought of as her people. Slavery was an abomination that also had to end. Amy was determined to scour this inhuman practice from the face of the earth. Lamp would be the first of many who would die before her mission in this world ended.

Argos and her sister, Mary, must die if she was to save humanity from a terrible fate.

After arriving from Europe, Argos had made his fortune in the new world by growing cotton on the plantation he stole from its former owner after that owner disappeared under mysterious circumstances. Fellow plantation owners readily accepted Argos' explanation that the previous owner had fled to Europe after failing to make good on his debts. Argos generously paid for the man's passage back to his homeland and he assumed his plantation in exchange. Of course, these so-called facts were completely false. Amy knew Argos had killed the previous owner, burying the head and torso separately in his own cotton field.

Argos then had a copious supply of the fresh, iron-rich blood supplied by the many slaves on his plantation, but also from slaves of nearby farms. It also meant the number of vampires was growing exponentially all across the Confederate States of America, also known as the CSA, with Argos at the epicenter of death and terror.

Amy intended to control the supply of fresh victims from the source and restore the world to balance. At least as she saw balance.

In order for her plan to work, every existing vampire would have to be permanently dead. As a one-woman army, she had the impossible task of tracking and killing all Argos' victims and their spawn. It reminded her of trying to stop ripples in a pond after dropping in a pebble. She needed help, which meant she needed a plan.

First she must build her own vampire army. Edward Lamp would be the tenth member of this army.

Her concern was it had been over one hundred fifty years

since the Union failed to stop the Confederate States from over-running the country, so she had very real doubts about her own ability to stop Argos by herself when an entire nation had failed.

A more personal challenge she had to overcome was her remaining human aversion to taking human life. She abhorred killing the living.

Amy shivered at the memory of Argos sinking his fangs into her flesh, the wet sound of him puncturing her skin, his fangs tearing through the soft tissue of her neck, then the pain as they sank into an artery in order to drink her blood. She recalled the exhilarating mix of pain, ecstasy, and horror than ran through her as her lifeblood ebbed.

She also recalled the finality of the fading sight of the filthy room she shared with her sister Mary when the release of death finally enveloped her. At the time, it seemed good to die.

The next thing she remembered was the warm, coppery taste of blood passing between her lips and the musty scent of iron in her nostrils. When she finished drinking her prey's thick life force, Amy sat back on her haunches on the straw mattress to discover, to her horror, she had killed her beloved sister.

Mary's stare at her with unseeing eyes still haunted her. Mary's motionless form, not breathing, a pale, waxy apparition, the side of whose neck was a ragged mess of torn skin, veins, and the oozing red wounds where Amy's fangs had ripped Mary's flesh was fresh in Amy's memory.

Gripped by the shock and horror of what she had done, Amy grabbed handfuls of her own hair and ripped them out, then threw back her head as a scream ripped from her lungs. Her body was wracked by deep, bone-shattering sobs as salty thick tears began to stream down her cheeks forming muddy rivulets on her cold, dead skin.

Yes, Amy would never forget Mary's ugly death until, in

what seemed like only minutes but could have been hours or even days, her sister gasped and began to breath once again. Amy watched Mary's breaths coming in short gasps as the wounds closed around tiny, round scabs of healing flesh. Mary's undead eyes slowly opened to reveal yellow eyes like those of a cat. Then her lips parted to reveal elongated incisors.

Mary licked her lips as her eyes narrowed and her once-dead gaze focused on Amy. "Hello, sister, should we feed?"

Amy realized immediately her beloved sister had become like Argos and herself. She had made Mary an undead monster spawned from hell. Her sister's death was on Amy's head. Now it was Amy's responsibility to end her beloved sister's immortality.

Unlike her sister, Amy had chosen to become a vampire. Her free will had resulted in a living death until the end of time.

Amy could have simply allowed the sun to dissolve her dead flesh, but so far she'd been unable to take her own life. What little humanity remained within her didn't want to die, not completely.

The irony was that once her humanity disappeared, the need to kill would be all she would lust after. All thoughts of her former life would be overwhelmed and she'd no longer be human. She'd witnessed these phenomena before.

Amy closed her eyes and shuddered at the image of the inhuman monsters she'd seen wandering the grounds of the plantation at night. Argos forbade his minions to attack his slave stock, but his neighbor's slaves were fair game.

Many slaves were reported missing but the humans assumed they had run off—a not uncommon occurrence with all the abusive plantation owners.

Posses of heavily armed men had been organized to locate the missing slaves, but so far none had been found.

Amy smirked to herself. She knew where Argos' prey slept

during the day, but the humans would never believe her if she told them. After all, she was just another slave and vampires were a myth. The other still-human slaves thought she was a voodoo woman, so they avoided her as if she had the plague.

The buzz of an air patrol not far away and coming from the direction of the Hoover Mountains made her tense and sucks in a breath. Her eyes shot open and she shifted her gaze to look at Edward Lamp, still lying prone on the grass. Lamp hadn't been resurrected yet and there was no telling how long it would be before he arose.

This could be a problem.

Using her ability to see in the dark as if it were midday, Amy scanned the stands of trees ringing the perimeter of the meadow. She grunted when she found the perfect spot. A cave in the side of a hill would be the perfect place to store Lamp until he was resurrected. Amy would need him and she wasn't about to let the CSA Police have him, not when her plans were so close to nearing fruition.

Grabbing Lamp's body, she tossed him over her left shoulder and carried him to the cave. Just after they entered the cover of the cave, a beam of white light lit up the meadow as if it were midday rather than two in the morning, forcing Amy to cover her eyes with her arms. The real sun would rise in just over three hours so she hoped the air patrol would have moved on well before then.

"Amy Selkirk," said an amplified voice, "we know you're there. Reveal yourself."

Doubts invaded Amy's consciousness, causing her to hesitate. How had they found her? She had been careful to mask her movements and hiding places during the daylight hours. Maybe someone saw her take Edward Lamp?

If she failed to respond, no doubt the CSA Police would begin carpet-bombing the meadow. The bombs would definitely kill her but would also destroy Edward's corpse and she needed him the world needed him alive a little longer. Until the rebellion ended Argos was the eye of this hurricane of terror. He would be the last to be destroyed then vampirism would end forever and the CSA would be finally defeated.

"Turn off the light and I'll come out," Amy said, shouting to be heard over the roar of the air car's twin turbines that held it aloft on a cushion of air.

The pilots must have heard her because the searchlight blinked out leaving only the craft's soft, indigo running lights to illuminate the meadow.

The air car then floated to the ground, landing on its tripod undercarriage, the engines' roar quickly diminishing, then stopping altogether as the craft came to rest on the grass.

The side cargo door swung upward on hydraulic arms accompanied by the soft whir of the motors. Immediately two armed CSA police troopers burst out onto the squashed grass, dressed in head to foot gray and green battle armor, the faceplates closed, their automags scanning the area around them ready to fire on anyone foolish enough to attack.

From bitter experience, Amy knew the troopers' weapons were loaded with rounds that would shred her into fleshy ribbons of bloody meat that even her ability to heal would be useless against. The CSA had learned the most efficient method to destroy a vampire without holy water or wooden stakes. Those ancient weapons against the undead were a thing of the past. Why risk close and personal? Why not kill from a safe distance?

Amy shuddered as she recalled several friends who had been shredded by CSA weapons, their flesh peeling off their bones, then burned to ash as she watched in horror. And Argos standing beside her, a sly grin on his lips as his police force murdered her friends. The choking stench of burnt flesh still filled her nostrils, accompanied by the wisps of charred remains carried by the wind, created by the swirling fires that seemed to invade every orifice of her body and cling to her clothing for days after.

Amy's eyes flitted to Lamp, who had yet to arise; then she stumbled out of the cave mouth, walking toward the two heavily armed police troopers with their weapons trained on her.

Her breath caught in her throat when she saw Argos, dressed in his usual head-to-toe black clothing. His shoulder-length, slick, shiny black hair was pulled into a tight ponytail revealing his angular features. He stepped out of the air car with her sister by his side. Mary's yellow eyes glinted in the running lights of the air car.

"Mary?" Amy said after coming up short. Her heart beat hard and her hands trembled. The old fears and doubts re-surfaced from deep within her.

Amy had sworn revenge when she learned Argos had planned from the beginning to make her change her sister into one of the undead. And she vowed to free her sister from the curse she had inflicted on her. Argos detested love in all its forms, even between siblings. His intention all along had been to make an example of the two sisters to the rebellious slaves by having Amy curse her beloved sister, Mary, with vampirism, demonstrating anyone could be made to turn on anyone, even their own beloved ones.

A knot of pure hatred burned within Amy as Argos, with a knowing smile on his thin, bloodless lips, his manner cocky, approached. Her hands formed fists at her sides and she fought the urge to strike out at the bastard.

"Hello, my dear," he said in his deep voice as he and Mary drew near.

Amy wanted to tear him open and gut him like a melon but she held back when a furtive glance at the troopers confirmed they still had their weapons trained on her. They'd burn her down before she could finish one step toward their master. She knew they were also vampires so their reflexes would be as good as her own.

"Hello, Argos," she said, her eyes shifting to look at Mary's ash gray face, then back to lock eyes with Argos. She was determined not to show him any fear or surrender to his will. With herculean effort, Amy had thus far managed to retain a portion of her humanity, making it difficult for Argos to control her, and she vowed to never let him control her or anyone else again.

But she also knew eventually her free will would disappear with her humanity. She fought against his power as much as she was able, but being this close to him chipped away at her inner defenses like a pick at a block of ice.

Argos reached into the pocket of his knee-length black pea coat and withdrew an ivory pipe. Placing the tip between his lips, he extracted a shiny, gold-plated lighter from his other pocket and after lighting it used the yellow flame to light the tobacco in the bowl of the pipe. He puffed and the contents glowed as smoke rose from the pipe. Amy could smell the rum-soaked tobacco.

After putting the lighter back in his coat pocket, he placed his free hand behind him and stared at her, puffing on his pipe, his inky gaze studying her. A sense of unease grew inside Amy with each passing second of silence.

Finally he spoke. "So we seem to have reached an impasse, my dear Amy. I gave you what you asked for and then you betrayed me. Is this the way for one of my children to garner my favor?"

Amy snorted. "You made me kill my sister...turn her into a monster..." Her voice disappeared behind a wall of rising anger.

Argos' brow furrowed and his eyes became hard. He tapped out his pipe into the grass, some of the embers still glowing, then placed it back in his coat pocket. She could sense his seething anger. "Amy, you're planning an insurrection against me. That is a violation of my trust and very disappointing."

Amy froze, startled by his words. She realized he should have killed her as soon as she appeared from the cave but he hadn't. Why?

"I should be dead...we all should be..."

"I think you know better than to say such a thing to me." Argos moved closer to her, giving the impression of him swooping down on her as if he were a bird of prey, which in a sense he was.

Amy took a step backward but in her mind she decided to stand firm. She glanced at her sister, who had an expression of wonder on her face that mingled with fear in her eyes. Then Amy looked back at her now furious former master.

It occurred to her that his anger made him weak; he had not realized he had stepped within her kill zone. She was about to throw caution to the wind and launch herself at Argos, intending to tear out his throat, when a man's voice from behind her caused her to hesitate.

'What's going on out here?" It was Edward Lamp, finally resurrected from death.

Argos stepped out of Amy's range as his features relaxed. "Nothing of consequence, my dear friend." His deep voice heavy with sarcasm. "You are just in time to see me deal with a traitor."

Amy turned her head to look at Lamp. "He means I'm a traitor for buying into his plans to change the entire world into his personal vampire army with him as absolute ruler."

Lamp, a big man over six feet tall, with broad shoulders and muscular arms, smirked. His thick body was now primed with the additional physical strength that came with becoming a vampire. He strode across the meadow, his wide face becoming more serious with each step. Finally he stood between the two armed troopers. He swept them both off their feet with his massive arms. They landed hard on their backs and lay still as their guns slipped from their grasps.

"I may have just changed the odds," he said, grinning at Amy.

Amy's eyes narrowed as she shifted her gaze to Argos, whose eyes were wide. This was something he hadn't expected.

Instead of fighting them, Argos turned and ran for the air car, which had already started its engines. It took off as soon as Argos had leapt aboard, the door closing behind him.

Coward, thought Amy.

"Thank you, Lamp," she said, turning to face her newly minted creation. "I'm sorry I turned you, but as you saw, it was necessary." Or at least she hoped he realized the severity of the situation.

At the end of the day, Lamp would have either been made a vampire by her or by Argos. It seemed he appreciated her cause, especially seeing how Argos had reacted to his sudden appearance.

"So what is the deal between you and Argos?" Amy asked Lamp as she moved to wrap one arm around her sister's shoulders. Amy was pleased when Mary didn't flinch but instead pressed her body against her side.

Lamp emitted a deep-throated chuckle. "I've never liked the son of a bitch. More than once I threw him off my land when I caught him sniffing around my slave huts."

Amy's stomach tightened at his use of the word slave. She'd momentarily forgotten this man had been as despicable as any owner of enslaved human beings.

The grin slowly faded from Lamp's square-jawed features as his expression became serious and his eyes narrowed. "I knew what he was and I wasn't about to let him take any of my workers. I treated them well and protected them from the bloodsuckers as best I could." He shrugged slightly, then continued. "Argos swore to kill me but every time he appeared I managed to drive him off. I used fire, wooden stakes, crosses, garlic...everything at my disposal to stop him." His brow furrowed. "Of course, now that I'm one of you, I don't know if I'll be able to continue protecting my people."

Amy's breath caught in her throat and her heart seemed to skip a beat. "What do you mean, your people?"

"I'm one quarter black on my grandmother's side. I inherited the plantation and vowed to treat the workers fairly and pay them. So far I've been able to keep my promise."

Amy's mind whirled with uncertainty and doubt. He could be lying. She had never heard of a plantation owner in the CSA paying slaves. Why had she not heard of this? "You're lying," she said, firmly convinced her words were true.

Lamp's wide face reflected his anger and his large, meaty hands formed fists. "No, I'm not." Amy watched as the anger in his eyes slowly faded, his features relaxed, and his fists unclenched. "I had to keep what I was doing secret or the other plantation owners would have told my buyers, who would have had me blacklisted. Not that I'm that concerned about money, but the loss for my workers would be far more than my personal fortunes would be able to afford." He sighed and turned his back to her as a breeze sprung up carrying with it the scent of the pine trees north of the meadow.

What Lamp was saying actually made sense. Amy made a decision knowing time was growing short. Argos wasn't about to let her get away again. He would end this once and for all— as far as he was concerned, at least.

"Lamp—"

Lamp turned back to face her with a grin on his lips, his gray eyes sparkling. "Call me Ed; everyone does."

Amy smiled to herself. She had taken a liking to this big man. "OK, Ed. I'm going to stay here with my sister. I urge you, beg you, actually, to continue the fight I started to destroy Argos."

Ed Lamp didn't say anything for several seconds, his eyes flitting between her and Mary. "What about you two?"

"Argos has no doubt ordered this area to be carpet bombed. In fact, I don't think you've got much time to make it to safety before a fleet of air cars arrives. Mary and I will stay behind and act as decoys so you can get away."

His words suggested he'd agree, but Amy needed to know for sure. "Ed. Will you do as I ask?"

Ed's eyes became hard and he nodded, his mouth a grim line of determination. Amy was satisfied.

As if to confirm his acceptance of her mission, he then stepped up to take her right hand in his. "I wish you well in the next world." His now sad eyes shifted to Mary, then back to her. "Both of you."

With those final words, Ed Lamp released her hand and ran toward the tree line, soon disappearing into the darkened tangled forest of trees beyond.

Amy watched until Ed was out of sight and she couldn't hear him in the brush any more, then turned to focus her attention on Mary. Moving to stand in front of her sister, Amy put her hands on Mary's shoulders.

"What are we going to do?" asked Mary, her eyes curious.

A single tear ran from Amy's left eye down her cheek. "My unnatural immortal, I'm about to release you from the curse." Amy swallowed hard. "But don't worry, we'll see each other again soon." The iron scent of Mary's tainted blood filled her nostrils as she bent closer to her sister's ivory skinned neck steeling herself to deliver the killing bite.

"Oh," was Mary Selkirk's last word as Amy sunk her fangs into her sister's neck and ended her undead existence.

Her sister's body sagged in her arms as air escaped Mary's lungs for the last time; the sound was quickly drowned out by the roar of multiple turbines that shattered the meadow's tranquility. The police fleet of air cars had arrived to bomb them into the next world.

Amy's heart was finally at peace as the bombs began to fall, secure in the knowledge Ed Lamp would exact revenge for not only her but for the countless people suffering from the curse placed on them by Argos and his undead horde.

# PROJECT PHOENIX

Russ Crossley

**H**uman history becomes more and more a race between education and catastrophe. - H. G. Wells

APRIL 17, 2021

Its thoughts flowed through his mind.

It knows everything.

An alarm warbled through the empty corridors of the underground installation deep below the Oregon desert. All sensation disappeared as the room was lost to a black void, a starless night. Silence. The remnants of the alarms echo washed over him. Secure. Nothing in, nothing out.

In the stifling darkness Ira Newfeld slid down the wall, his sweat soaked back slick against the cool porcelain tile. He sat statue like on the lab floor. The only sound now was his own breathing as he felt another malodorous trickle of sweat run down his lean face. The others are finished.

A heavy pounding began that came from the secured inner door of the testing room. The door, composed of two inches of hardened steel with re-enforced hinges, meant it wouldn't be able to get to him.

General Walters ordered the evacuation. Too late. Now they were all gone, he was alone and Ira knew he needed to let someone in the outside world know before it was too late for him.

He froze to listen to the sound of tortured steel being rendered followed by the crash of the door slapping hard against the tiled lab floor. Then all sound again ceased. Ira's heart beat furiously in his ears.

"Ira," a whispered voice called his name.

Ira held his breath a scream caught in his throat. He knew then he wouldn't be warning anyone about what was happening here.

"Come out, come out, wherever you are," whispered the voice in his mind. He listened to the muffled echo of footsteps that moved slowly toward him.

---

IF YOU WANT TO MAKE AN APPLE PIE FROM SCRATCH, YOU must first create the universe. - Carl Sagan

JANUARY 25, 2023

"They're all dead," says President Romana Wilson, her voice flat.

I'm stunned. "Everyone?"

I'm in a window less conference room with the president and two men I don't recognize. The walls are decorated with paintings of various presidents dating back at least two hundred years. The table is twenty feet long and the room large enough for the cabinet to hold their meetings. But there are only us four present.

President Wilson nods to indicate I should take a seat then crosses her arms across her chest, her gray eyes flicker as I sit across from her. Her tan suit looks like it's been pressed and her yellow blouse is the color of spring daisies in bloom.

MY stomach knots. Since I'm the only scientist attending this meeting it means I'm all that remains of the original Phoenix Project team. I know why she wants me in particular. Whatever she's up to involves the infamous project, and its hell spawned offspring, and I know with absolute certainty I want no part of it.

"I want nothing to do with any project involving Phoenix. I thought I made that clear..."

"Oh, we won't be going back to that again." The look in her eye says she's attempting to bait me and it works.

"I don't understand..." I say my eyes narrowing as I gaze at her shimmering image. She turns and speaks softly to someone off camera then turns again to face the camera.

"Rather than just telling you, how about I show you?" She smiles at me her eyes hard. I'm about to object and tell her there's no way I'm leaving the Lark when she must've guessed what I was about to say because she says, "Before you jump ship I'll have a presentation you must see then you can judge where we go from here. Okay?" She arches one eyebrow.

I indicate my agreement with nod. The president smiles grimly then she shifts her eyes to one of the silent men and indicates with a wave of one hand to proceed. The lights in the room dim then the holo-presentation begins. What I see makes my jaw drop. It's the end of the world, at least for the human race.

When the presentation ends, the room is suddenly cold

even though I know the temperature controls haven't been altered. The image shimmers again and Romana stands before me only this time she's leaning against her desk with her arms crossed across her chest, her expression grim.

"Bill, I know how you feel about this, but we have a real problem on our hands and we need your help. I mean it, Bill. Without the intervention outlined in the presentation the human race will die out within fifty years."

I gaze at her dumfounded by this news. I'll be dead by then but so will everyone man, woman, and child on the planet. "Romana, I will help if I can. I don't know though if we have time."

She nods and the tension in her shoulders visibly relaxes. "The project is called Brahma, after the Hindu God of creation, headquartered in a small town in Oregon."

I gaze at her overwhelmed by a sense of puzzlement. The sides of her mouth curled up and her mouth forms a slight smile.

"Don't worry we've set up a fully equipped laboratory and staffed it with the best of our remaining geneticists..." she pauses to take a breath and the slight smile fades and her eyes become hard. Obviously something she hasn't said continues to upset her. "You and Dr. Khanna will be sequestered there until you have perfected the technology to stem this threat. The two agents I dispatched will take you to the lab so you can begin work."

The holo-projector goes dark startling me with the abrupt termination of the image. I'm wondering who or what is this Dr. Khanna?

"Olsen and I'll wait here, sir while you get ready," says World Security Institute Agent Paul Watson with a smug expression on his young face. He's obviously pleased that the first part of their mission is successful. The clone cops are an impatient lot. The two agents delivered the message-holo from Romana.

I change into my softest blue jeans, worn red and blue work shirt and my favorite walking shoes, the brown leather ones, very comfortable for long trips, and pad again into the hallway.

I'm met by the two agents in the lobby. They stand the moment they see me and I detect they're anxious. I note the way Watson glances at his watch when he sees me and I realize that his calm, take your time demeanor is a cover for his urgency.

I shrug, why should I give a shit about their timetable? "Okay, guys let's haul ass." I hook my thumbs off the pockets of my black jeans.

---

JANUARY 26, 2023

Wisdom begins in wonder. -Socrates

THE SALTY WIND HITS ME FULL IN THE FACE WHEN I STEP OUT of the limousine onto the potholed gravel parking lot. The drive from Portland International took two hours too long for me. I already hated the place even before I got here, wherever in hell here is. A ragged looking seagull screams as it floats into the strong wind overhead, that comes toward me full force off the wild ocean. The vast horizon is consumed by white-topped surf. A long stretch of gray beach runs north and south as far as I can see. What little grass grows on the embankment is sparse and the color of dry straw.

The shack that stands in the middle of the parking lot is dilapidated and seems ready to collapse under its own weigh with one more gust of raw wind.

I pull the dark knee length raincoat Agent Watson gave me on the plane tighter about me. "How am I supposed to work in there?" I shout to be heard above the howl of the wind.

"That's an elevator building, doc. The lab is below ground." Watson waves me toward the structure. I shrug and follow him, after all I've come this far why not at least see the place?

Once inside the building, the outward appearance being a clever deception, the wind stops. The reception area, staffed by an armed guard who sits granite like behind a wall of surveillance monitors stands as we enter. He requests our identification. Watson gives me a temporary security pass with a digital picture he'd made during the flight affixed to it. I feel the guard's eyes on me as he studies the picture then my face, at least I now know what a microbe feels like. He slips the card through a scanning device, the strip on the back is encoded with my DNA, and there are two indicator lights, one red and one green. The red light comes on after he's run my card.

He looks up, with a look of someone very serious about their chosen profession, and hands me back my card. "Thank you, sir."

The guard repeats the procedure with Watson and Olsen, two more red lights and we're cleared to proceed to the lower levels. A color-coded chart next to the elevators doors tells me that the underground portion of the facility below ground contains over thirty levels.

"Where are we going?" I ask. Watson turns his head slightly to glance at me and a small smile crosses his lips.

"To the bottom." He points to the purple floor on the chart with one index finger then turns away and presses the down button. I feel a vague sense of unease as I stand between the two agents. I'm about to go way over my head, literally.

---

WE'RE GOING TO TURN THIS TEAM AROUND 360 DEGREES. - Jason Kidd

. . .

My mind so whirls with possibilities that I fail to notice our stop at the lowest level. The doors slide open and we step into another lobby, the walls glow white, back lit by rows of florescent bulbs. Another uniformed guard stands behind a reception desk recessed into the floor identical to the one at ground level. His swarthy, grim features study us as we approach and I note his eyes travel over our security passes then our faces his eyes examining ours for any sign of trouble. These guys are careful.

"Watson, WSI." He motions toward me. "This is Dr. Lumberman."

Then guard nods silently then plucks a hand held communicator from the desktop and speaks softly into the device. Even though I am close to him I fail to make out the words.

It isn't long before a brown skinned man wearing a wide smile appears from a hidden door in the wall behind the stoic guard. He is dressed in a black turtleneck, blue jeans, and brown leather loafers, his lean form covered by a knee length white lab coat.

Above the lab coats breast pocket is a plastic nametag that tells me he is the mystery man of the hour, Dr. Khanna. I smile and take his firm grip in mine.

"Dr. Khanna, where's your badge, sir?" says the guard giving the new arrival a disapproving glare.

Khanna shrugs and reaches into a pocket of his lab coat and pulls his identification badge. The guard nods obviously satisfied. Khanna grimaces at me. "We all need to wear them. Sorry, it's nothing really just can't be too careful."

Khanna leads me through the door. Watson doesn't follow us so I assume his job was over for now. Much to his relief I'm sure.

Once inside I'm shocked to see the number of work stations each with its an electron microscope, protein synthesizer, protein sequencer, DNA synthesizer and DNA sequencer. The sophistication of this laboratory is truly impressive I don't recall ever seeing such compact technology in a genetics lab before. At the end of the room, which I estimate is the size of a football field, and equally as wide, is a wall made of smoked glass that separates the lab from another room. The room on the other side of the glass must be dark, because no light escapes from the inside.

The lighting in the lab itself comes from rows of florescent tube boxes hung from the ceiling. The light box covers diffuse the light to give the room a gentle haze like quality.

I move to the first station and gaze at the sophistication of the gene sequencer. The compatibility of the new models is inspired genius compared with the much larger one I worked with during the Phoenix project. One thing bothers me though.

"Dr. Khanna, this is all very impressive, but why so much equipment?"

Khanna smiles warmly and crosses his arms. "That didn't take long." He sighs heavily. "Dr. Lumberman..."

"Bill, please..."

"Of course...Bill." He continues, "We modify gene sequences to build a better human by adding foreign DNA —"

"That's bull shit." I interrupt him. "We tried that during Phoenix and it failed. Every time we tried to introduce a new gene other than human the sequence became non-viable, no matter what the type of DNA."

Khanna shrugs. "Yes I know, I read the research, but what if I told you we found a way safely introduce foreign DNA that works."

"I'd say you were a liar."

Dr. Khanna's dark eyebrows go up and he grins, with a twinkle behind his eyes. "Is seeing believing?" I nod.

"Well then, Bill, follow me." He turns and heads away toward the wall of smoked glass. I follow gripped by curiosity. What he's talking about is nonsense science. I wonder where

Romana got this guy? I didn't seem to recall reading his name in any of the serious journals. Maybe he's one of those self-professed *experts* so often quoted in the supermarket tabloids.

I stare at the wall of dark glass unable to see anything on the other side when it begins to swirl as if churned into motion be some unseen whirlpool. Larger swirls form in the glass wall and the smoke begins to dissipate. Light begins to show through until there are patches of clear areas forming. Finally I see what is hidden on the other side. There is a woman seated at a clear glass table eating a bowl of soup. I can see the steam rising from the red liquid (very likely tomato) as she spoons the hot soup into her wide mouth, between full lips. She wears a brilliant white jumpsuit that covers her lean body and her poker straight hair is the color of motor oil, sleek and long falling about half down her back. Her eyes are a brilliant green, unusual for someone with such dark features. She must be no more than twenty years old.

It's difficult to tell what her ethnic background is, she looks part Asian, Slavic and Italian all in equal proportion, strange yet exotic at the same time.

"This is Kya," says Khanna his eyes glow with obvious pride.

I watch her for a few minutes noting her vacant stare at the wall, no looking side to side, no interest in anything but a blank wall. She doesn't even seem to be interested in the soup. With one hand in her lap while the other spoons each spoonful of soup with mechanical precision then the spoon drops to the bowl ready to take its next excursion. Not one drop is spilled during this process.

"Is she alive?" I ask.

Khanna chuckles. "Of course she is, she's our test subject. Don't you recognize her?"

My eyes narrow as I study the young woman. I shake my head.

"Bill, she's the only viable embryo left from the Phoenix

project. We needed a baseline for the new generation you and I will construct under the new program. She's worked out very well, yes, very well indeed."

My skin grows cold. "You mean you took one of my genomes? We destroyed them."

Khanna shakes his head.

I watch the young woman for a few moments unable to speak, the words caught in my throat, finally I say, "Let's say your telling me the truth, which I highly doubt until I see the data, and let's say this woman is a fully realized clone from a marriage of human and foreign DNA, what is the difference between her and the last generation of clones."

"Bill, didn't you read the reports I sent with Watson?"

"No, I don't read reports I like to see the facts for myself."

Khanna faces me and frowns. "Hmmm...that's unfortunate." He pauses. "It's like this; we were able to adapt extraterrestrial DNA to enhance this woman. She's a hybrid and much a more advanced human being than has ever lived."

---

EVERY GREAT ADVANCE IN SCIENCE HAS ISSUED FROM A NEW audacity of imagination. -John Dewey

To say I'm in shock is the understatement of all time. Romana's presentation said human DNA is breaking down due to the high pollution levels in Earth's ecosystem.

We're on the brink of poisoning our environment and ourselves out of existence. The technology to move our people to another planet doesn't exist so we were about to disappear from the universe forever. The presentation ended by saying that Project Brahma, without any specifics, will create a new breed of human that will adapt quicker to the future biosphere and extend our lives until the environmental problem was overcome by new technologies, but alien DNA? Were these people nuts?

"Where did you get the alien DNA?" I say. We're seated at one end of a long steel table in the automated cafeteria being served our dinner by one of the servo-bots. The room is large enough that our voices echo off the walls. I'm eating broiled gen-chicken with a side salad and Dr. Khanna (who urged me to call him Marty, an Anglicized version of his real name Momar) a vegetable curry. The pungent curry smell permeates the room preventing my enjoyment of the chicken. It's a shame really they certainly don't serve anything this expensive at the Lark.

"Actually I don't know." He looks embarrassed by his lack of knowledge.

"You mean to say you introduce a foreign life form into our DNA not knowing where it originated and the possible ramifications?"

He nods and his eyes drop to his plate of greenish curry.

I feel the anger begin in the pit of my stomach. These people are playing with fire and they don't even seem to care. I decided to withhold judgment until I've reviewed the data. "Let's see the records after dinner."

He nods again unable, or unwilling, to make eye contact.

After the servo-bots have removed our dishes we head for the lab to review the data. The wall of glass is fogged again, though having seen the wall become translucent I am able to discern the swirls of dancing rainbow of color that now obscures our view of Kya. As I sit behind one of the workstations, and the computer monitor lifts from a hidden compartment that appears in the smooth black surface of the station, I hear a strange voice echo in my mind. It's as if a fleeting breeze has crossed my thoughts brushing against me. I shiver from the mental touch. Maybe the lab is haunted.

Dr. Khanna sits on a three-wheeled stool off my left shoulder watching me. His long arms are crossed.

"So, Marty, why all these stations for just the two of us?" This had been bothering me since I arrived.

"There were twenty-seven members of the project team working here when I joined the project." Getting this guy to give up information is like breaking your leg just before a once in a lifetime vacation, you just want to scream.

"Yes, but where are they now?" I hold up my hands to show I wasn't getting it.

"Dead," he says in an unemotional tone.

I whirl in my seat to face him. His brown eyes are watery. "What? How?"

"She did it." Now normally I would assume he meant Kya expect she looked about as benign as the clone cat at the Lark.

"Surely not Kya."

His brown eyes abruptly came up to fix on mine. I knew immediately. Somehow that exotic young woman killed the entire project team, but...

"How did they die?"

"Two years ago. Their minds were eaten."

"Eaten?"

He nods. "That's about the only way I can describe what happened to them. When the security force managed to get into the lab they found the corpses untouched, no blood, no signs of violence, Kya was the only survivor, other than Ira Newfeld."

Newfeld? That surprised me, but why only him?

Marty continues to explain, "During the autopsy I ran some detailed memory scans on the bodies, you know with the new ones that show the last forty eight hours before the memory engrams lose integrity then they fade. I discovered the memory receptors were empty. Everything wiped, gone. I coined the term, eaten."

"Where's Newfeld?"

Marty shakes his head his eyes drop away. "He died two days

after he was retrieved. Probably for the best really, he was in pretty bad shape. What was left of his mind was barely enough to keep his organs functioning. He didn't have the wherewithal to hit the self destruct switch."

I gaze at Marty and he glances at me and shrugs. "I'll show you where the switch is later, just in case."

I don't appreciate his lackadaisical attitude but what am I going to do? I'm here and I have to do something to save the human race. My concern right now revolves around Kya and her mysterious abilities.

I decide to change tact, "Is Kya a telepath?"

Marty stares at me, his face twisted by conflicting emotions. "How do you know this?"

"I felt her."

Marty smirks. "Now who's the liar?"

"I felt something or someone brush my mind."

"Impossible."

"Why?" Now we are getting somewhere.

"I installed a chip to control her telepathic ability. She cannot..." he pauses and his eyes narrow. "I will make sure," he says curtly.

Marty shows me the emergency panel where the autodestruct switch is located. It's a rather mundane looking black button on the panel that might be connected to the lights for all I can tell, not that I know what to expect it to look like. Maybe I expect the word 'DANGER' in big red letters, or something, the only label underneath the switch says ERT (and in tiny letters beneath it, so small I need my reading glasses to see them, it reads Emergency Response Tracker). Marty tells me that once activated the entire laboratory complex will be open to the sea within seconds and everyone inside will be drowned. The walls contain thousands of baseball size ducts, which lead to the Pacific Ocean, barely twenty feet from where we stand. I feel a sense of unease at this bit of information and immediately gain respect for the nondescript switch.

After this I return to my quarters to rest. I lay on my single bunk staring at the ceiling trying to absorb what I've learned today.

If Kya is a hybrid of human and alien then what do we need her for? And more importantly what do they need me for? They seem to have her under control. I feel a sudden jolt run through my body as a powerful mind touches mine.

They need you to make more of me and solve the telepathy problem.

I feel as if I'm losing my mind but I respond to the voice. "How is telepathy a problem? I don't understand."

You will. Silence. I expect the walls to cave in any second but nothing happens.

I make my way to the lab and fail to find Marty. Where could he be? I walk up to the wall of smoked glass and the swirling mass of color begins to dissipate. I see Marty lying face down on the floor inside the enclosure. I start as I see Kya, her dark eyes study me as if I were the fish in a fishbowl.

He's dead, says the voice, which I knew to be Kya's.

"Why?"

Like Dr. Newfeld he thought I was his private guinea pig. I am not.

"That much is obvious, Kya, but did he deserve to die?" She shrugs her narrow shoulders and a small smile crosses her full lips. I feel as if I'm in a trance, mesmerized by those two tepid pools of green. I know what I must do. I have no choice. If I fail the horror of what Khanna...no, what I, created will be set loose upon the world. It seems that the end of the human race is inevitable, a testament to our arrogance. I struggle against her mind as I make my way along the wall to the emergency panel. My finger hesitates over the switch that will end my life's work. I feel the invader grip my mind and my body shakes with wave after wave of torment she rains down on me. With a rush of realization I know now why they need me. Romana and the damned clone cops know I'm the only Phoenix member left with a conscience. I'll make the correct choice.

They know I'm the only person on Earth willing to stop Kya before she's able to rip my mind away. They know I have abilities that no one else has, damn them. I don't want to do this. My hand trembles while rivers of sweat obscure my vision as I reach for the switch.

Have to stop her. I will...

It knows.

It ends.

---

For of all sad words of tongue or pen, the saddest are these: It might have been! - John Greenleaf Whittier

Nineteenth day of 47th year the Order of Jera
Excerpt report: Survey 13781, Leader Motal Telo:
Latal sector the third planet, Zon class star.
Damage to ecosystem as follows:
Scans confirm, planetary atmosphere unable to support life.
Life improbable given the current conditions.
Recommendations:
Abandon research project this sector until ecosystem self repairs.
Next survey: 160th year of the Order of Kir.
End report.

# LEGACY OF THE HUNTED

Russ Crossley

I shifted the prey's weight in my arms, then lowered it onto its back on the rain-slicked blacktop of the trash-strewn, stinking alley. It blacked out quickly after I squeezed its airway closed. I was careful not to kill it. Not yet. My food is best eaten fresh.

Not that it's heavy. I caught it at an awkward angle when it fell backward is all.

My nose wrinkled under the assault of a putrid mixture of sweat, stale booze, and excrement (not all of it human) wafting around the prey like a cloud of misery. I had let it drop the final few inches to land with a wet smack on the pavement. I stood over it and watched the chest rise and fall with each breath.

It would be better off dead.

Its unkempt grey beard and shoulder-length, white hair reeked of drain cleaner. Like a lot of the street rats, the older ones boil off alcohol in the brand of drain cleaner favored by the addicts. The local merchants stock enough of the killer cleanser to clean the entire city's drains. Damn leeches make money off the misfortune of others.

I shrugged. The cattle's business is none of mine. I feed on them, I don't judge them.

Back in the day, my father raised chickens. He never asked the chicken its opinion before he loped off its head.

But sometimes I can't help dwelling on who I am and where I come from. When I do, I begin to think like I did in the twenty-first, in the days before I became a vampire. Life as the undead in this century can be challenging. Two hundred years is a long time, and a lot has changed.

There used to be others of my kind, hunting on these dirty streets. But in the past fifty years, I haven't encountered a single bloodsucker. Back in the day, I would sometimes join forces with other vamps and we'd herd the prey together as if we were a pack of wolves. The group hunts ended in thrilling orgies of blood and death. Those days had been awesome.

Today the hunt is a loner's profession, so I don't think about the old days much anymore. When I crave rich, fresh blood, my memories fade like a morning mist. Not that I've seen a morning in a long time. In fact, it's a memory that is badly faded.

Back in the day, humans still believed in the supernatural and good and evil. These days, the humans worship science instead of God. They don't believe in the undead. They think vampires are a myth from bedtime stories and all I am is a simple serial killer. Perpetuating this myth is my greatest disguise.

I knelt next to my kill, tilted its head back to expose the pale throat, and then sank my fangs into its yielding flesh. The warm, life-giving blood immediately flowed down my throat. I drank until I sensed the old one's heart had stopped.

I stood and ran my index finger around my mouth to wipe

the excess blood off my lips, then sucked the remnants off my finger as if it were an elixir. I closed my eyes and purred my satisfaction, savoring the moment.

Old blood is the best. I estimated the prey's age to be at least forty, maybe even a little older. A good vintage.

My hunting grounds are separated from the cities of the rich and powerful by a twenty-foot-high, burnished-steel wall. The wall is topped with an electrified fence, and has automated guard towers at six-foot intervals brimming with deadly fire-power. A single bullet hurts; three hundred rounds per second will shred my body into rags. It's difficult to come back from that type of damage.

More than a hundred years ago, the poverty-stricken and the drug and alcohol abusers were herded to this side of the city and kept here, fully expected to die young. Which they usually do with or without my help. As humans are wont to do, the poor and disenfranchised have breeding habits that are reminiscent of the rats that scurry about these dark streets.

As I see it, my job is to cull the herd. The rich and powerful need me.

On those occasions when I visit the other side of the wall, I witness how the rich and powerful humans live.

Extreme wealth gets you genetic manipulation to create the best bodies money can buy, and rejuvenation technology keeps those fortunate enough to have the price of young-and-beautiful alive for up to two hundred years. There are rumors that they've broken the resurrection barrier. Soon the humans will become immortals.

If this rumor is true, it means the Nosferatu are obsolete. Who wants to be immortal if it means you are an undead hunter of blood when science delivers the same results without the complications of bloodsucking and possible death-by-stake?

It's tough when you're the one born in the wrong century.

Today I sense something's very wrong. A scent reminiscent

of an old danger lingers in the air, descending on me like a gray death.

I am the last of my kind. When I die, there will be no more vampires. I could have made more vampires, but why? I don't see any future for my kind.

The eternal struggle between good and evil has been swept aside. A new legacy is about to be born to replace the old ways.

To replace me.

---

I SIT UPRIGHT IN THE ROTTING WOODEN COFFIN LEFT VACANT by the destruction of my vampire master, Rumsfeld.

Over one hundred years ago, my master, Albert Rumsfeld, died at the tip of a stake wielded by a vampire hunter calling himself Vengeance.

The hunter moved with inhuman speed to stake my master before he could react.

After a titanic struggle, I killed the hunter by impaling him with the very stake he planned to use on me. Though I triumphed, I was shocked to discover Vengeance had genetically enhanced superhuman strength far greater than normal humans.

Since that day, I've worried when I will encounter another genetically enhanced superman such as Vengeance. I worry I may not defeat the next one. But I haven't seen another of his kind since.

"Welcome, my mistress." Peter, my loyal servant, stepped from the shadows into the fading daylight across the cracked and stained cement floor. The retreating sun casts a chaotic pattern of jagged light, formed by the remains of the glass in the broken basement window.

Peter is my most recent blood-slave. He's blond and young, no more than nineteen, with thick, muscular arms and legs.

He's dressed in the rags common on this side of the wall. His addiction to designer heroin is forgotten under the influence of my deft touch. After I bit him, our blood mingled. Now he hovers between life and death, ready to do my bidding. I've made him a better man by saving him from the curse of addiction.

"Any word from Alicia?" Climbing out of the coffin, I stand barefoot on the rough cement floor.

A thin smile passes over Peter's lips. He nods.

"Be ready to brief me in a few minutes." Dismissing him with a wave of a hand, I watched him shuffle into the deep shadow until he sat again on his stool. I smiled inwardly.

I love having a blood-slave. It's so cool being powerful.

As is my practice, I did my daily stretches in the nude. The early evening air was thick and heavy with humidity, but I didn't sweat. Not that my ageless, undead body needs exercise, but I've been doing morning stretches since I was fifteen years old and I'll be damned if I'm stopping now.

When I finished, I ran my hands through my curly, ink-black hair to smooth the more unruly hairs and moved to a scarred wooden chair where I had thrown my clothes before going to sleep.

Alicia Dickson is my spy on the other side of the wall. Her mission is to scout for the threats I know are coming and to alert me to impending danger. I took extreme risks to obtain fresh clothing for Alicia.

Alicia is the daughter of the director of city security, who has a soft spot for his only daughter who somehow recovered from her syntho-heroin addiction. She is the perfect mole, and the perfect slave.

I quickly dressed in my black leather pants and matching top until at last I pulled on the flat-soled leather boots that rise halfway up my calves. The leather is cool against my skin.

"Peter. Tell me the news."

Peter rose and walked to stand in front of me, his hands folded in front of him, his handsome features placid. In another life we could have been lovers, but such human-centric urges have long ago vanished from my consciousness.

Peter turned, reached down, and retrieved a white cardboard box tied with string sitting on the floor next to his stool. It reminded me of a cake box.

"What is it?"

"A gift from Alicia's father." Peter's voice trembled ever so slightly. Without my enhanced senses I never would have noticed Peter was upset, and my internal warning bells were going off.

He handed me the box.

I held it by the string, which I used to carry it to my coffin. I closed the lid with my free hand and set the box on top of the polished oak casket. I broke the string and slowly opened it. What was inside the box was not a cake.

Inside was Alicia's dismembered head.

---

I SLIPPED INTO THE SHADOWS IN THE ALLEY JUST AS A surveillance droid appeared from a doorway. There were a lot of droids on the street tonight, far more than is the norm. They're hunting for something. I hope it isn't me, but deep inside I know exactly what they're seeking. A vampire named Lilly Ames. Me.

A pair of gunmetal-gray droids appeared at the other end of the alley, floating above the brick roadway on their antigravity streams. Suddenly the alley became as bright as high noon. I covered my eyes until they adjusted to the sudden intrusion of light. Normal light doesn't harm me.

Good thing they weren't using infrared lights.

Of course, the humans don't believe in vampires anymore. It

wouldn't occur to them to install special lights just for me. They think I'm a serial killer. A mentally defective human on a killing spree.

I blinked to clear my vision and waited for the droids to act but they stayed frozen, sweeping the alley with light. It was as if they were waiting for something, or someone.

"Madam," said a shrouded figure, who stepped between the two hovering droids. His eyes were hidden in the shadow created by his wide-brimmed hat. I knew this human's a male because the voice was deep and thick. This human has strength and confidence.

A twinge in my gut signaled me to be cautious. My nostrils twitched. This man smelled of danger. He is what's been bothering my senses.

His square jaw was covered with dark stubble and he wore a western style duster right out of the old west. I saw he even wore black leather cowboy boots. Finally he tipped his head back to reveal obsidian eyes that scowled at me from beneath the brim of his well-worn hat.

The guy's a cliché right out of the twenty-first-century vampire movies.

Is he kidding?

I immediately scolded myself. I had to be cautious and control my impulse to rush at him.

I let the left side of my mouth curl upward and my eyes narrow. I braced my legs and prepared for the attack I was certain was coming. My acute hearing detected the movement of air behind me and I realized two droids had taken up positions to prevent my escape. Not that this would work.

"What do you want, hunter?" I asked in a low growl. My fangs extended.

The hunter took two steps forward and swung aside the right side of his coat to reveal a holster with the butt of a pistol showing.

"You think bullets will kill me?"

I was surprised when he shook his head.

"No, of course not." A slow smile spread across his chiseled features.

It dawned on me that this man knows what I am. My gut tightened. His gun had to be loaded with silver bullets. As if reading my thoughts, he swept aside the other side of his coat to reveal a row of four wooden stakes in leather loops hanging from his belt.

"Coming from a costume party?" I asked, my voice leaden in my ears.

He shook his head again, this time slowly, his dark eyes never leaving mine. "No. I'm a vampire hunter."

I snort. "Vampires? Who believes in such fairy tales?"

"More like nightmares, actually." With inhuman speed, he snatched a stake from its holster and hurled it at me in one smooth motion. It cut the air with a swish, racing for the center of my chest.

The distance separating us was no more than fifty yards, so the wooden missile covered the distance quickly. Without my enhanced reflexes, I would already be dead; but with a flex of my legs, I sprang upward to the rooftop of one of the buildings bracketing the alley. One of the droids immediately captured me in a bath of light. I stood on the edge of the roof, gazing down at the hunter looking up at me.

He didn't look surprised. This worried me.

"Nice move." He chuckled and crossed his arms. "Thank you, Lilly, you've just confirmed what I told him."

I cocked a single eyebrow. "Confirmed what to whom?"

The hunter removed his hat and bowed. He stood straight as his generous mouth formed a wide smile. "Let me introduce myself, Lilly. My name is Malice. You were acquainted with my late brother." His eyes narrowed. "Until you killed him, of course."

I stared at him and slowly I began to realize who he was. I recognized that face, but it was impossible. He's dead. I killed him a hundred years ago.

---

I PACED THE BASEMENT, STOPPING OCCASIONALLY TO STARE AT the pile of bones lying in one corner of the room. The rotting wooden stake still sticks out from between the age-brittle rib cage. The flesh had long ago rotted away and the rats had scattered the small bones from the extremities like the feet and the hands to who knows where. The upper torso, hip and leg bones, and the skull are the only larger bones still intact. But the real point is he's dead.

I killed him.

I stopped pacing and slapped the flat of my hand repeatedly against my right leg and folded my bottom lip repeatedly. It's like I'm ten again.

Is Malice a twin? I shake my head.

No. My senses say otherwise.

He's real. They must have resurrected Vengeance to come after me. But why give him a new name?

And he knows my name. How?

I turn to glare at Peter, sitting quietly on his stool, his features placid as always. I recall Alicia's sightless blue eyes staring up at me from within the box. The dry brown blood pooled around the severed neck. Her death came suddenly. A very sharp blade was used to remove her head.

The style of her execution bothered me. A story told to me by my master came to me. I stroked my chin with my long fingers and tried to recall Albert's tale.

Albert loved to tell stories about his days as a member of the undead. He'd been a vampire for six hundred years before he made me. I had been the atypical innocent, blushing bride, nineteen, on her honeymoon with her new husband, Kelly.

I smiled grimly at the memory of that day, then walked to the window to stare at the sliver of moon visible through the shattered window. I remember that night better than any other.

Without warning, Albert came out of the shadows and sank his fangs into Kelly's neck. I recall being frozen with fear, watching the life in Kelly's pale green eyes slowly fade as he died. His last breath left him, his eyes rolled up to reveal the whites, then he collapsed like a puppet with its strings cut.

I willed my legs to move but I couldn't move, a scream caught in my throat. Unable to speak, unable to move, unable to scream, I watched Albert come at me, his eyes red as if a reflection of the fires of hell.

I felt his cold breath on my neck, then the searing pain of his fangs as they pierced my vein. I recall the blackness creeping in from the edges of my vision and my body becoming weak. Albert's strong arms held me up as I sank into a black abyss. I remember wondering how such an old man could be so strong. Finally I passed out.

When I woke I found myself in this basement, propped in a corner. I raised my head and saw Albert seated on a stool, his arms crossed over his sunken chest. His flesh was white as a bone and his clothes looked old-fashioned, yet still new.

His red-rimmed eyes stared at me. Then he stood over me with his arms still crossed. "How do you feel?"

I blinked and moved first my legs, then my arms. "Surprisingly good."

He chuckled dryly. "You, my dear, are now one of us."

Albert explained that he was a vampire and rather than killing me he had made me a vampire. I would live forever and never age.

Now for a narcissistic gal of the twenty-first century, this sounded pretty good. When I asked about Kelly, Albert seemed truly sorry he'd been unable to save my new husband. To this day, I think he was lying.

At first I resented Albert, but he was my master so I let it slide. Over the next hundred years, I learned all there is to know about my life as a vampire from him. In my own way, I grew to love him.

The story that twigged my memory involves a nineteenth-century vampire hunter named Barnabas Sloan.

Sloan's weapon of choice was a saber he used to sever a vampire's head. Besides wooden stakes or silver bullets through the heart, removing a vampire's head does the job nicely. The trick is, the head must be buried separately from the rest of the body, ensuring the vampire would not rise.

In some traditions, the vampire's headless corpse would be burned to ashes.

Did Barnabas Sloan kill Alicia?

If the common link to recent events is Sloan, then I have a chance. His deathblow is to use the sword. This is a close-in weapon. I've lived for two hundred years and have been instructed by a master vampire. I have the advantage.

But I'm worried. If it is Sloan, then he sent Alicia's head as a message. I eyed Peter and it dawned on me that his earlier nervousness was out of character. He had information I needed.

My hands dropped to my sides and balled into fists.

---

BEFORE PETER DIED HE TOLD ME EVERYTHING.

Alicia's father commissioned a research project to resurrect a nineteenth-century vampire hunter and, worse, to clone him after the public saw an image of me killing a prey. They doctored the image to make it appear I killed a rich citizen when in fact my kill was a homeless drug addict on this side of the wall.

Her father sought revenge after he discovered Alicia was my blood-slave. And they found a way to chemically nullify my blood-slaves and turn them against me. I broke Peter's neck after he told me that.

Vengeance had been the result of an early experiment to clone a vampire hunter. The clone was enhanced with super steroids making him strong and aggressive.

The disappearance of Vengeance resulted in the project being shut down. Eighty years later, a new series of cloning experiments resulted in an army that over the past fifty years hunted and destroyed the vampires, all except me.

Of course, the big game changer is that the elite have finally achieved immortality. They no longer need me.

Worse yet, they successfully resurrected Barnabas Sloan and made several clones designed specifically to hunt for me. One is called Malice.

A thump from the room above startled me. I glanced at the window and quickly realized I had no more than an hour until sunrise. I needed a new hiding place.

Peter must have been implanted with a homing device. Malice was upstairs and he knew I was here.

My hunch was confirmed when I heard the soft pad of his boots starting down the stairs and the hum of a droid guarding the top of the staircase.

My body tensed as I waited for the basement door to open. The footsteps stopped on the other side of the door.

"Lilly, don't attack. I need to speak with you." It was Malice, all right.

"Why should I trust you?" I call back.

"Because Alicia told me about you."

At the mention of Alicia, I decided to let him enter. There was something in his tone that I trusted, something I'd sensed earlier in the alley. He didn't lie, or maybe he was a poor liar.

Whatever it was, for the first time in two hundred years I decided to give a human a chance. Before I killed him.

"Come," I said simply.

The door creaked as it opened and Malice stepped into the room. He wore a lopsided grin on his narrow features and his eyes sparkled with amusement. He was dressed as before in the costume of a nineteenth-century hunter.

"Lilly. It's so good to see you again."

I crossed my arms over my chest and glared at him. "Say what you came to say."

His grin dissipated and he swept his hat off his head in one smooth motion, releasing a nest of brown curls that fell around his face. He moved to my casket and placed the hat on the lid.

"I've come to you with a proposal." His soft brown eyes locked with mine.

"Oh, and what might that be?"

He swept the right side of his duster aside and slipped his thumb over the heavy leather belt. His pistol was absent.

He must have noticed my look of surprise because a brief smile passed over his lips. "As you can see, I'm not armed."

I considered killing him immediately, but for reasons I cannot explain, I hesitated. This proposal he spoke of intrigued me. "Go on."

"Barnabas proposes you work for us."

I cocked one eyebrow. "Work for you?"

"Yes, as a vampire, of course."

I dropped my arms to my sides, chuckled grimly, then moved closer to within easy striking distance. I didn't see the fear in his eyes that was usual just before I sank my fangs into humans. This man had no fear.

"Before you kill me, I must tell you the immortals want you dead. They've hired Barnabas and me to do it."

"But in a few seconds you'll be dead, then all that's left is

Barnabas." I emitted a deep growl. Malice didn't move and his eyes remained placid.

I sighed and took a step back. "All right, so what do want of me?"

"You and I and Barnabas must form a syndicate. Without each other, we are all dead. None of us is meant to be alive in this century. We are an infection to them. The immortals plan to eradicate this infection beginning with you, then us, and then they will eradicate all humans considered imperfect." He drew out this last word.

I realized immediately what he was telling me. Without a vampire to hunt, two clones of a nineteenth-century vampire hunter would become redundant. They needed me to exist and I needed them to exist. We are codependent. He's right.

"So, what's the plan?"

---

I HAVE AN APARTMENT IN THE CITY NOW, AND I HAVE A JOB.

I kill for hire, for food, and for self-preservation. Barnabas and Malice control the city through terror and assassination, with me as their instrument of death.

The first human I killed for Barnabas was Alicia's father. I enjoyed that one. I cared about Alicia. Her father deserved to die.

I even have a new blood-slave, an immortal named Randy. He'll be with me forever.

The legacy of the hunted has shifted from me to my prey. The immortals make an excellent food supply. For the first time in a long time, I'm looking forward to the next two hundred years.

# END OF THE FLIES

Russ Crossley

Tonight, just as I sat down to dinner in front of the TV, my wife, Merle, starting screaming and running around the house. Naturally, I ignored her.

This crazed behavior had been happening every couple of days over the past month. I've tried a few times to assure her the sky wasn't falling, but she just wouldn't believe me, so I gave up.

When she ordered me to drop the newspaper I was reading. To help me ignore her, I kept reading. Yes, I ignored her.

Why you ask? She'd done this too many times and it was driving me a little nuts.

Problem is this time I should have paid a little more attention. This time she was cursed up the yang-yang, and we (meaning all of us) were in real trouble. Fortunately, some of what was upsetting her managed to slip through my husband-filters.

Over the past month she's told me stuff like the government know about a Texas-size meteor about to hit the Earth and wipe us out, but they were withholding the information because we'd all panic. If Texas really was about to land on my head I know I'd certainly be freaked out.

This piece of paranoia crapola came from her hairdresser, an eighteen year old kid who read it on a conspiracy website.

Then there was the inevitable alien invasion. This came from her brother-in-law Albert before they carted him off to a rubber room upstate.

No, Seattle wasn't about to be invaded by little green men, or white sexless beings with big bald heads and eyes proportionally too big for their oval faces (whether they were male or female remains a mystery).

But today there was a new twist. Today she complained some guy, calling himself Mope something (I don't recall the name exactly), walked into the mayor's office demanding the mayor let Mope's people go, or else.

His people? Who has people anymore? These days not even a Wall Street banking executive claims they have people. (And if they do, they keep it on the QT).

And what was this or else stuff? Since my wife is the executive assistant to the mayor she's usually plugged into such things, but she had no idea what this Mope guy was talking about. And, she added, neither did Mayor Billy Ramses.

That was until the curse changed everything.

I flicked the channel changer to the five o'clock early news and turned up the sound. I was sitting with my TV dinner on the aluminum TV tray with the shaky hollow aluminum in front of me, as usual. On the screen the perfectly sprayed and combed channel two news anchor, Peter Hasting, the man with the perfect white teeth, started his newscast in the usual way.

For the past five years he always starts with a flirty joke with the weather girl. But today, for reasons that will become obvious, he suddenly froze in mid-punch line and stared wide eyed into the camera. His face actually changed to the color of wood ash. Not an easy task with all the makeup those guys pack on their kissers.

I've seen him use this particular dramatic tactic many times, to increase the suspense of the story to follow. I watched all this half-interested in this so-called Big News Development.

"We take you now to Lake Washington where there is breaking news."

"What no tagline? Com'on, Pete, 'ol buddy. Hook me, baby." I spoke at the television, then snorted in disgust, before I stuffed a large forkful of greasy chicken strip into my mouth.

Peter's tone had that deadly earnestness reserved by local news anchors about to report the birth of a new cow to farmer Jones and family. What a maroon.

I glanced at Merle seated to my left in her matching wing chair with her TV dinner on the tray in front of her. She hadn't touched her food. No loss there really, the chair probably tastes better.

I did think it odd that her cheeks were damp with tears and her hands were trembling. I rolled my eyes and turned my attention back to the television in time to see an aerial shot of the lake. It sure looked red. Strange. The sky visible in the background was still as blue as ever.

I chuckled around my mouthful of stringy chicken. "Hey, Merle. Will ya look at that? They broke out the helicopter to report the birth of a calf."

I shook my head then crammed a fork full of the glutinous mash potatoes with the artificial chicken gravy into my mouth. At least I wouldn't have to chew the stuff.

I realized Merle was right not to eat this crap. I grunted and stuck my fork into the rubbery so-called bird meat then shoved the tray away.

A dyed blonde female reporter appeared on the screen

standing on the lake shore. "Thank you, Peter. This is Lori Oldsby reporting from Lake Washington—" I snatched the remote from the end table next to my chair and thumbed the off button. Lori and the crimson colored lake disappeared into blackness.

I got up from the chair, stuffed my hands into the pockets of my tanned Dockers and began to pace back and forth in front of her.

"Ya know, Merle, sometimes I wonder why we stay in this town. I mean we eat TV dinners for supper every night. You work seven days a week for that walking penis of a mayor. And I'm in a dead end job I hate. I mean how long will it be before China takes over the aircraft manufacturing industry. Five years? Ten? Boeing can't last forever ya know. We should move somewhere else."

"I'm cursed," Merle said softly.

I stopped pacing, placed my hands on my hips, and turned to face her. Strange why was her skin green? Maybe she wasn't feeling well.

"Are you okay?"

"I'm cursed," she repeated, only this time her voice had an edgy rasp to it. I must admit it was kinda sexy actually.

"Oh, really? What is it this time? Aliens? The Loch Ness monster? Dracula? Zombies? What?" I snapped my mouth closed. I was shouting.

I crossed my arms over my chest and let out a breath. My frustration with the way she'd been acting for the past month had finally spilled over.

"Sorry." I closed my eyes and whispered, "It's just all this stuff you've been saying lately is driving me a little nuts and —" I opened my eyes and looked at Merle.

Oh crap!

She was brilliant green and a long forked tongue flicked out of her mouth. I don't recall her having a long forked tongue, but it's surprising how a flicking tongue can be a real turn on, even when your wife is turning green.

"Ribit!" she croaked. Her body shape changed before my eyes. She was now sitting on her haunches like a dog. Or a frog...a frog! My wife had become a large frog!

"What's going on here?" I glared at the frog. "What have you done with my wife, hoppy?"

The frog responded with a deep croak again then leapt off the chair leaving behind a pile of Merle's clothes. Now my wife the frog was jumping around our living room naked. What if someone else came into the room right now?

I slapped my forehead with the palm of my hand. What was the matter with me? My wife is a frog, for goodness sake. A frog.

My eyes narrowed. This had to be the work of that Mope guy she talked about earlier. This had to be the or else.

But how do I find him? I certainly wanted my Merle back. And just to be clear Merle the human, not the Merle the frog.

***

AFTER I PICKED UP MERLE AND PUT HER IN THE CAB OF MY pickup I drove to city hall. Along the way I passed groups of frogs. They were everywhere. In the designer clothing shops, coffee shops, dry cleaners, hairdressers, jewelry stores, book stores. Everywhere. But the weird thing was there were men frantically trying to catch them. Every time they managed to catch a frog it slipped out of their hands and jumped away.

What was going on? Had the whole world gone frog-centric? Was there a frog convention in town? Now I was being paranoid. When your wife turns into a frog it sure messes you up.

Then it hit me like a foul ball at a Mariners game, there were no women on the streets. Only men and frogs.

Like my Merle, had all the women changed into frogs? But why frogs? Was this Mope guy responsible? Or was it someone or something else? Was it aliens, or swamp gas, or a government experiment gone wrong?

I certainly didn't have any answers. All I had right now were questions. I only hoped her boss; Mayor Ramses would have some the answers.

When I arrived at city hall the guards who were normally at the entrance to the visitor parking lot had disappeared. As I passed the guard shack I noticed two uniforms lying in heaps on the floor, as if the guards had stripped them off and dropped them right there.

I pulled into an empty stall in the lot and turned off the engine.

"Ribit!" Merle croaked at me from the seat beside me.

"Yup, we're here, babe. Don't worry, I'm gonna find a way to make you human again, or my name isn't Rusty T. Quits."

A fly that had been trapped in my truck flew by Merle. Her dark eyes followed the path of the insect then suddenly her long tongue flicked out of her wide mouth and snatched the fly in mid-flight. And just like that the fly disappeared inside her mouth.

"Ribit," she croaked again. She seemed happy to have the bite-sized snack, but I was horrified.

Oh, crap. When she gets normal again how am I going to tell her she ate a fly with her tongue?

I keep a canvas tool bag in the bed of my truck in a locked box. I got out of the cab, with Merle resting on the flat of one hand. I then climbed into the flat bed and unlocked the steel box. I emptied the tools from the bag and carefully placed Merle inside. She didn't protest or try to jump away. I thought about saying, 'Good frog' but it would just sound stupid and condescending to a woman in her condition.

Still her big black eyes gazed at me seemingly trustingly.

Before I zipped the bag shut I assured her everything would be fine, though I had serious doubts.

"Hey, pal you talkin' to the frog?" said a man's voice behind me.

I slowly turned around to discover a man with hair the color of snow dressed in all white from his shoes to his suit jacket. The corners of his mouth were curled slightly upward. Was he mocking me? I hate being mocked.

I scowled uneasily. "Like, yeah. I'm married to the frog so watch what you're saying about her, pal." My day had so far gone so badly I wasn't about to take any crap from anyone, and especially not from a guy who sells garbage bags for a living. Not even if they're good garbage bags.

Now he smiled. "Sorry. No offense meant. It's just that I've met a lot of people today married to frogs, or their girlfriend are frogs, or their best friends are frogs." The smile disappeared. "It's been a strange day."

I nodded then stopped and studied him for a second or two. "Who are you anyway? I've been to city hall many times, and I would remember you."

Both of his white eyebrows rose on his forehead. "Oh, do you work here?"

"No. My wife does." I stuck one hand in the pocket of my Dockers and picked up the tool bag with the other. "Well, she did until...you know." I sighed. "Somehow I don't think they'll keep her on as the executive assistant to Mayor Ramses now that she's a frog."

"Mayor Ramses," blurted the garbage bagman, suddenly excited. "Your wife works, sorry, I mean worked, for the mayor?"

"Huh, yeah, sure...why?"

He came up to me and draped a long arm across my shoulders and began to guide me to the steps leading to the lobby doors.

"My friend, you and I can do each other some good."

"Who are you anyway?" I asked again.

He chuckled. "Teamsters, Local 4402, Sorcerers, Magicians and Spirits Union. I'm the organizer for Moe Sheppard. Jacob's the name. I'm his right hand man. Your wife ever speak of us?"

I shook my head. "No, not really." The guy behind this was named Moe not Mope. What an idiot I am. I had gained new respect for my frog...uhhh, I mean my wife.

But, magicians? Sorcerers? If my Merle ever became human again I'd never doubt any of her crazy conspiracy theories ever.

"So you know this Mope...I mean, Moe guy who threatened the mayor?" I asked hopefully.

We were just outside the twin glass doors to the city hall lobby. We stopped short, too short and I nearly fell forward, but he held me tightly. I'd annoyed him.

The last thing I wanted to do was piss off a magician, or whatever he was. I could be the next one turned into a frog, or something worse like a rat or a pig. I couldn't imagine spending the rest of my days wallowing in garbage and mud.

Jacob's arms dropped to his sides and he frowned at me. "The teamsters union has no knowledge of any threats real or imagined ever being expressed or implied to anyone."

"Ok, ok, let's not go all Senate-investigation. It's just two good 'ol boys talkin'. I'm only repeating what Merle told me."

Jacob's eyes narrowed. "Who's Merle?"

I rolled my eyes. "My wife. Like I said she's a frog, but I love her, warts and all. She's my frog."

Jacob grinned. "Of course she is. No worries, pal." Somehow I'd become his pal again. "Let's go inside and meet with the mayor and Moe. They're in talks right now."

I studied him. I didn't trust the guy. He seemed a little too slick, like a used car salesman. But then again what did I have to lose? And maybe I could talk this Moe guy into making Merle human again.

I shrugged. "Yeah, ok. Lead on, MacDuff."

He looked at me quizzically, like a dog when it's confused. I'd found his Achilles heel. He didn't comprehend clichés. "It's an expression meaning take me to your leader," I explained.

Jacob shook his head. "Okay, if you say so."

I smiled to myself and followed him through the glass doors into the carpeted lobby. Score one for the janitor.

---

WE ENTERED THE MAYOR'S OFFICE WITHOUT KNOCKING TO find Moe and Billy Ramses silently glaring at each other from opposite sides of his large glass topped desk. There wasn't anything on the desk between them, not even a scrap of paper, never mind the computer monitor I'd seen on Billy's desk the last time I was here. As I recall that was about a month ago, just before started Merle her conspiracy rants. At that moment I could have kicked myself for not believing her.

"Hey, Billy," I greeted the mayor as I set the tool bag on his desk. He glanced at me and nodded without saying anything in return. It was like watching a staring contest, or paint dry.

Billy's jowly features were pasty and his chipmunk cheeks were ruddy. His blood pressure must be about ready to explode.

Moe looked over at me. His arms and face were deeply tanned and his build was reminiscent of an NFL quarterback. Six foot four inches of solid muscle, with a dimple at the end of a wide chin, sure intimidated me.

I've always pictured magicians as gnarled, stoop shouldered old men who wore pointy hats and flowing robes so this guy was a complete surprise.

So much for the Hollywood cliché. I offered to shake his hand by sticking out mine.

Moe smiled at me and stood. He took my hand in his and I was glad when he didn't squeeze too hard. I winced and struggled to not show the pain. The triumphant look in his eyes told me I'd failed. He released my hand and let it drop to my side. The circulation would come back, eventually.

"Hi, Moe Sheppard," he said introducing himself. I couldn't place the accent. Maybe he was Icelandic. I'd never met an Icelandian before.

"Huh, Rusty T. Quits."

"Tquits? Is that French?"

"No, it's T period Quits," I explained, "and it's Polish, on my father's side."

He smiled. "So you come from a family of Quitters is that it?"

I was beginning to take a serious dislike to this guy and I'd just met him. "No, we're Quakers actually. We don't believe in violence." I looked him straight in the eyes. "But there have been exceptions."

He smiled smugly. I wanted to slap him, but since he out weighted my by at least thirty pounds of muscle, I decided to let it go.

"What can I do for you, Quits?" he asked.

"I'd like to talk to, Billy. Privately."

Moe shrugged. "Sure, why not? Mayor Stall-tactic and me have been getting nowhere. Maybe you can talk some sense into him."

Moe and Jacob left us alone saying they were going to the cafeteria to get some lunch. They'd be back in twenty minutes.

Once we were alone I sat in a chair across the desk from a weary Billy Ramses. "Billy, tell me what's going on around here. All the women in town have been turned into frogs." I opened the tool bag and Merle jumped out to land on the desk.

"Ribit," she croaked and blinked repeatedly under the glare of the florescent lights.

"Get that thing off my desk," said Billy raising his voice an octave.

"Billy, this is Merle."

"Oh." He collapsed back into his leather executive chair, a defeated man. He undid the top button of his white dress shirt and loosened his red striped tie.

"They want me to let their people go," he said, bitterly. His eyes were locked on his desk.

"People? What people, and where are they going?"

He looked up at me, his brow creased. "The union wants the city to pay for two weeks in Hawaii every year for all their members. I can't agree to that. The taxpayers would lynch me."

"And who would that be exactly, the frogs, or the husbands of the frogs?"

As if a light bulb had suddenly gone off his features relaxed. "Ya know, I never thought of that." He reached into his suit jacket pocket and pulled out his cell phone. "I should call my wife."

"You mean your frog?"

He stopped his index finger hovering over the numbers on his phone. "Ya know, I never thought of that either."

I wondered how this moron ever got elected. "Billy, what you have to do is agree to their terms and get back your wife and mine and the rest of the taxpayers. It's the only way. Okay?"

"I could nuke 'em," he said.

I shook my head. "No, Billy only the President can order that, and besides who ya gonna nuke, union headquarters?"

"Oh. Ya know—"

"You never thought of that either?" I finished. He nodded sheepishly.

---

A FEW DAYS LATER AT HOME IN MY LIVING ROOM, WATCHING the five o'clock news, with Merle beside me on a new love seat as we watched the five o'clock news snuggled together. (Human Merle that is, not frog Merle).

Peter Hasting was speaking. "Alien space ships have landed in Washington. Preliminary reports are they are demanding we turn over all potatoes..." I reached for the remote and turned him off.

As the screen went dark I looked at Merle. "What do ya think?"

"Anything's possible," she said. I nodded.

Her brow wrinkled. "What is it?" I asked.

"Have you ever had hunger cravings for something weird?"

"You mean like flies?"

"Yeah. Weird, huh?"

I smiled. Yeah, if I hadn't convinced Billy to give in to the unions demands it would have been the end of the flies for sure.

I only hope Moe and Jacob were enjoying Hawaii.

# FIVE MINUTES

Russ Crossley

Bump looked up from the newspaper he'd been studying into the green-gray eyes of the red haired waitress standing staring expectantly at perfectly cut auburn hair did nothing to disguise she was older than she wanted to be. The oval patch over the sagging left breast of her white uniform blouse read Thelma. He assumed this was her designation.

Bump considered it sad that in his line of work the only women he met had to work past their expiry date and were usually damaged goods. His was a rotten business and some-times he really hated it. But this particular job meant he had to locate another type of woman. A woman with a deadly agenda.

Only he hoped the woman he'd been paid to find wasn't as world weary as this one. If she was then she wouldn't care about her life or anyone else's. These type of targets were the scariest kind. He really hated those jobs, but a guy had to make a living didn't he?

"What'll it be?" she said her voice rough from too many smoke breaks.

Sometimes he'd forget how many people smoked in the twentieth century. In his day no one smoked. Smoking had been banned long ago.

Too bad he hadn't time before he left to have dummy tobacco sticks made up. He'd have to say he didn't smoke which would put his cover in jeopardy each time he said it. His recollection from his college history class about the middle of the twentieth was everyone smoked. Children as young as five or six started smoking, then they were hooked until they died of smokers cough. At least that was how he remembered it. But he could be mistaken, he wasn't much of a student

Regardless, his plan was he'd be out of here before he had to tell anyone he didn't smoke.

"How 'bout your phone number?" He hoped she didn't say yes because he'd never used a telephone and he had no idea right now how long he'd be in this time.

Her gray eyes narrowed and her mouth formed a sneer. "'Aint on the menu, buster." She stuffed her pad and pencil into the pocket in the front of her apron tied around her waist. She turned around and retrieved a white coffee cup from a stack on a counter under the stainless steel pass bar that separated the cook from the waitress.

On the other side of the open pass bar was the white haired cook in a white cotton undershirt. He sported two missing teeth and hadn't shaved in a couple of days evidenced by the uneven gray stubble on his street weary face. An angry scar ran across his chin and up the left side of his face.

Thelma cocked an eyebrow at him. "Coffee?"

Bump smiled. "Yeah. Sure. Thanks."

She snorted as she turned her back to him. "Don't be thanking me until you've tasted this mud."

"You watch yor mouth, T," said the cook gruffly from the kitchen.

The coffee shop was empty at this time of day. Evidently no one fancied greasy spoon food at three in the morning.

Thelma smirked and selected a white porcelain cup from a stack next to the large steel coffee percolator on the counter then held the cup under a spigot and filled the cup with black coffee. She set the full cup in front of him. His nose wrinkled at the smell of over cooked beans cut with too much chicory.

He recognized the smell from his days in the marines when he was stationed in the outer worlds. They used to cheap out the military in those days. The days before the second Great War. A buddy who'd stayed in sent him an e-note once telling him how jarheads ate steak every night and drank gourmet coffee.

Bump never heard from the guy again so he assumed he'd become fodder in the seemingly endless war to end all wars. At least he left on a full stomach topped off with some decent coffee. Not like this foul swill was sure to taste.

He folded the newspaper in half and lay it on the coffee counter and searched the counter for the sugar and salt and peppershakers. There were none in evidence. "Sugar?"

"You're kiddin' right?"

He remembered now. Milk, sugar, flour and salt were rationed but he didn't remember why. And he couldn't recall at the moment who the enemy in this war had been. He glanced at the headline on the folded newspaper. Duhhh. Nazi's. Of course.

"Do you have any milk?" he said politely as possible

A sardonic smile played across her lips and she went to a large refrigerator standing at the end of the counter shoved against a wall next to the swinging door to the back. She came back with a glass bottle half filled with milk.

She tipped it and whitened his coffee. He smiled at her. "Thanks."

'Where you from, mister?" Thelma said when she came back from putting the milk bottle away.

Oh, oh. Now what? "Why would you think I'm not from around here?" he said keeping his voice as even as possible.

She eyed him suspiciously. "You talk funny and your clothes are wrong."

Bump sat back against the back of the chair and chuckled. "Well, well how 'bout that. Nothing gets past you does it, Thelma?"

She scowled at him and looked about to leap across the counter at him. He'd insulted her. He'd never been skilled at sarcasm. Not good. She'd soon begin to think he was a Nazi too.

"Sorry. What I meant was you're right. I'm visiting. I'm from Chicago." It was a lie but certainly preferable to the truth.

Thelma's features softened. "American, eh? What ya doin' here?"

"I'm a private investigator. I'm trying to locate someone. Name's Bump McShott."

Thelma turned her head toward the kitchen and yelled, "Hey, Archie, Sam Spade is in the shop."

"Tell him he's gotta order sumthin' like everybody else," called Archie from the kitchen.

Thelma offered him a thin smile. "Archie don't go to the movies much."

Bump wondered what a movie was and who how he'd been mistaken for a guy named Sam Spade. He thought about correcting her but her eyes had the spark that meant he'd found his way in to her camp. Problem was he had no idea what a movie was.

He made a mental note in future he should do better research before coming this far back. Unfortunately, this job's timeline didn't allow sufficient time to do the necessary research. All he'd been able to do was find a vessel to inhabit for the twenty-four hours he needed to track Pinky Ames and to stop her.

The time table said he'd only have five minutes after he found ted her but his one strong asset was over confidence born of success. It was why he accepted the hefty pay day, if he achieved the objective. His business was result based so it was feast or famine. And famine usually meant paradoxes for someone. So far he hadn't created any personal paradoxes, at least none he was aware of.

He smiled at Thelma and took a sip from the warm coffee mug. He winced when the acidic brew burned his tongue. He was thankful when his taste buds were burned because it meant he couldn't taste the stuff. He'd drunk coffee during other assignments and the stuff was an acquired taste he'd never acquired.

Thelma leaned her elbows on the counter and stared at him with a thin smile on her lips. "You're not from Chicago are you, Bump?"

He believed the popular jargon of the period in this circumstances' went; 'The jig is up.' He had no idea what a jig was but somehow it fit this situation. "No. Not Chicago," he said slowly, keeping his eyes fixed on hers.

Thelma straightened up after removing her elbows from the counter then crossed her arms over her bosom. "I know who you are because I'm also not from Chicago." She nodded toward Archie who was visible over the stainless steel pass bar in the kitchen. "And neither is Archie."

"What year?" Bump asked. It was along shot but something about the way they talked told him they were out of period too.

A shadow of a smile played across her lips and her eyes narrowed. "2434. You?"

"2418," Bump replied. "Kinda crowded in the past these days don't ya think?"

Thelma smirked. "Yeah. Sure is." Her brow wrinkled. "Corporate, government, or private?"

Bump set the mug on the counter then reached over ad pulled a paper napkin from the dispenser. He wiped his mouth with the napkin then crumpled it in his fist. "Private. Like I said I'm a private investigator."

Thelma's thick, dark eyebrows formed twin arches on her forehead. "Really? You really a PI?" He nodded. She chuckled and shook her head. "Me and Miles are on holiday. You sure look the part in that rain coat and the fedora."

Bump grinned. These two were rich morons on a lark.

Somewhere in their program was an automatic retrieval worm if they tried to change history. Any attempt to assassinate Hitler, or provide future technology to someone in the past resulted in automatic retrieval, a hefty fine and prosecution. There had been a few cases where the death penalty had been handed out but most often the offender was subjected to a memory wipe.

Since the entire purpose of vacation time travel was to see and interact with the past, and share the experiences at parties, a memory wipe was considered a sufficient deterrent.

The idle rich were the customers of the time travel corporations so they stayed in line with the rules.

Bump had lost count of the number of times he wished for a memory wipe, but while his trips were privately funded they were hardly vacations so he was allowed some leniency in the application of the rules. And the Time Enforcement Agency had thus far been unable to tie him into any disruption to the timeline. The corporations who hired him had friends in high places to take care of his missteps.

Bump reached into the pocket inside his suit jacket and pulled out a black and white photograph. He showed the smiling woman depicted in the photograph to Thelma.

"You seen her in here? Or has anyone mentioned an Arlene Bennett to either of you."

This diner was near the debarkation wharf where the troop and cargo vessels docked to refuel and load with men and material for war. Just about every sailor that had ever come through the port had come into this diner. Bump assumed this was why Thelma (obviously not her real name) and Miles (disguised as Archie) wanted to be here. They'd get a wealth of experiences from the sailors who came through to brag about at parties.

Surprisingly Thelma scoffed. "Archie, get out here."

She must have become accustomed to using her companions cover name because she sneered it in the sincere way people who believed what they were saying. These two had clearly done their research before coming back.

Bump stuffed the picture of Arlene Bennett back inside his suit jacket just as Archie came through the swinging door. A grease stained white apron covered his clothes and trails of dirty sweat streaked his puffy freckled cheeks. Sitting atop a nest of tight oil-black curls he wore a round white hat. His jaw was tight with undisguised anger.

Bump swallowed hard. This man was a tough customer.

Thelma looked at him with a sneer ion her face. "Throw this guy out, Arch."

"What? Why?" said Bump. He remained seated as Archie rounded the end of the counter and came at him. He realized he wasn't getting an explanation when Archie spun the stool around and grabbed by him shirt collar and his belt and yanked him to his feet. Spots danced before his eyes due to the sudden application of force to his windpipe.

Bump estimated Archie had a good fifteen kilos on him so he knew struggling would be pointless, and would likely result in a black eye or a broken bone or two. Any serious injuries would delay his mission and he'd miss his window of opportunity. Missing an assignment was unacceptable to his employer and would result in disciplinary action.

He smiled to himself. Too bad discipline meant a single shot to the head. Not that he was worried, his success rate of one hundred percent and holding was in the corporations and his best interest to maintain. The corporations didn't wish to attract unwanted attention from the certain government agencies if his assignments went awry. Of course he'd be the one to suffer the most but any corporation with a prohibition to mine the past would soon enter bankruptcy. The arrangement was symbiotic but deadly in its implications.

Archie raised so his feet no longer touched the floor and carried him toward the front door of the diner.

Bump gagged and sputtered waving his arms as the heavily muscled time traveler-slash-cook carried him to the door. Once at the door he was dangled in mid air for what seemed to be an eternity. His vision blurred as a lack of oxygen starved his brain. He heard Thelma heels click on the dirty tile floor until she came into view and swung the door open. She offered a tight lipped smile and waved her fingers at him just before Archie tossed him out the door where he landed hard on his butt on the rain soaked sidewalk.

He gasped for air and spots danced in front of his eyes as he managed to drag the first few breaths into his tortured lungs. Slowly his breathing normalized. His butt was wet and it hurt like hell.

His day wasn't going as he'd planned that much was clear. But unanticipated violence was in the job description.

After managing to stand on shaky legs he stumbled into the alley across the street from the diner. Daybreak was still several hours away so he had little concern he'd run into trouble in the alley.

With his mind now clear, Bump decided to stay where he was to observe who arrived in the diner after his abrupt departure. The alley was shrouded in shadow so he wouldn't be seen by anyone walking by.

In contrast the diner was well lit from inside. He would have a perfect view of anyone coming and going in the diner. Her saw Thelma and Archie moving about their movements frantic and nervous. They reminded him of birds in a cage. It seemed they had lost their courage after their rough treatment of him.

Right now they were looking mostly to the west toward a row of three story brick apartments farther down the street. Evidently, something about Arlene Bennett had unnerved them.

He didn't have to wait long because a woman wearing a scarf over her dirty blonde hair appeared huddled in a long wool overcoat rushing toward the diner. She entered through the diner's door. The echo of tinny bell over the door drifted on the cold winter air to him standing in the alley. He shivered.

Thelma and Archie who appeared highly agitated given how they spoke rapidly and waved their hands about as if to emphasize what they were saying immediately met the woman. Now he understood his treatment. These two were conspirators with Arlene Bennett and this woman had to be Arlene, the subject of his investigation.

Bump considered bursting into the diner and apprehending her but this would not stop whatever plans her employer had in mind, he or she would just send someone else. And he'd not discover the identity of the person who hired her. His information was a corporation had hired her, she wasn't an agent of an official body.

Now raised, angry voices drifted through the windows of the diner. Bump smiled to himself. His appearance had upset their plans. "Good," he mused under his breath.

Finally Arlene left the diner, after slamming the door hard

behind she walked briskly headed toward the row brick apart-ment buildings that abutted the dock area.

Bump stepped out of the alley and began to follow her keeping a discrete distance between them. He ducked into another alley when Arlene stopped to look for anyone following her. He held his breath and stole a quick look around the wall and to see she once again had started walking. He started after her keeping his distance and using any shadows he encountered to cover his tailing her.

They had walked nearly an hour and were in an area of the city unfamiliar to him. The buildings were still made of brick, mortar and stone but they were higher and more ornately deco-rated along the roofline with scrolls and carved stone statues of gargoyles and other mythic creatures.

Finally they arrived at the apparent destination because Arlene entered one of the buildings using a key she pulled from her coat pocket.

She closed the door behind her and he heard the echo of the lock being turned.

Bump waited several seconds then rushed to the door. As he suspected it was locked.

He grunted softly in frustration then scanned the street to see if anyone was watching him. Delivery trucks had started moving on the streets but there were no pedestrians on the sidewalks at this still early hour.

Looking back to peer at the lock in the door handle, Bump reached into the pocket of his overcoat and pulled out a small red disc-shaped object. He placed the disc over the keyhole in the door and there was a soft click. Taking one last look both right and left at the street and seeing no one he swung the door inward and, after pocketing the disc, slipped inside closing and locking the door behind him. He had to be careful not to let anyone of this period see the lock pick.

Since he had no idea where in the twenty story building

Arlene would be he decided to check the directory to see if he recognized any names from the thin briefing file he'd been provided. Naturally he'd used his usual back door sources to augment what he was provided, and to determine exactly who he was working for. He needed to know of the true objective of his mission.

Bump hadn't survived fifteen years in this business without discovering the hidden agenda of his employer. He was fairly sure every corporation that hired him knew he did this but they never said anything since he got results.

In the low light coming form the beginnings of dawn coming through the lobby windows he Bump scanned the names listed alphabetically on a brass plate set in the wall between the two elevators.

His heart froze and he took in a breath when he came to a name he recognized. Robert Shaw, MD, Room 1012.

Dr. Shaw was the ancestor of his employer, Hart Shaw CEO of Light Drive Technologies. Arlene was here to kill Dr. Shaw. But why?

---

WHEN HE ARRIVED AT THE OFFICE DOOR OF DR. SHAW, BUMP saw there was light coming from under the door. The rest of the building was deserted so this had to be where Arlene had come.

Resting his ear against the door he managed to make out muffled voices. Good. Arlene hadn't left so Dr. Shaw must still be alive.

Bump slowly tried turning the doorknob, but like the lobby door it too was locked. He cursed under his breath. The elevator motors broke the silence startling him. His heart beat rapidly and his mouth dried.

He was running out of time the early starters had begun to

arrive. Bump ran his tongue across his lower lips then took out the lock disc and placed it on the Dr. Shaw's door lock.

It was risky to burst into the room. If Arlene had a weapon trained on Dr. Shaw she'd kill him before he could stop her. And then his employer would be gone and then a paradox for him and death for a whole line of Shaw's and who knew how many others. He would need toy proceed with caution, even if it meant his own death.

Bump heard the lock disengage then he slowly swung to door in. The light inside went out.

"Hello?" he said as the door opened. "Dr. Shaw?"

"Come in and close the door behind you," said a husky woman's voice. It must be Arlene.

As Bump's eyesight adjusted to the low light coming through drawn shades over the windows the shrouded image of a someone standing next to a chair with another person seated became distinguishable.

"Dr. Shaw?" he said again.

"Dr. Shaw is tied up at the moment. What do you want?"

"Uhhh, I need some medical advice."

Arlene chuckled mockingly. "Yeah. Nice try. Dr. Shaw isn't a medical doctor so you may as well leave."

Bump smiled to himself. "Sorry, you and I both know I can't do that." Bump moved to the right side of the door and found a light switch on the wall. He flicked the switch and the overhead light in the middle of the ceiling. He blinked and recognized Dr. Shaw seated on a wooden chair. His arms were tied to the chair with black electrical cord and a cloth had been stuffed in his mouth. Bump recognized him because his future great, great, great grandson looked exactly like him.

He hadn't been harmed but that was about to change. On the floor underneath the chair was a bomb, a bomb he recognized. When it went off it would implode everything within five feet. Since it was designed to implode upward Dr. Shaw and the would disappear forever. It would be like he never existed which seemed poetic.

"How long?" he said simply gazing into Arlene's eyes.

Her eyes were dark as a pool of water at night and her expression was placid, unconcerned. Her attitude unnerved him. But he was determined not to show she'd gotten to him.

"It has a five minute timer. We have four minutes and thirty eight seconds to get out."

He knew exactly what she meant. They'd leave these bodies, that would be consumed by the blast, and their own consciousness would return to their own time. It concerned him that he and Arlene might not exist in the future since the timeline would have been altered, but that was the risk of corporate espionage in the past.

Sometimes he wondered what reality was anymore. With all the time travel going on reality had probably changed so many times that truth had little meaning.

He and Arlene could have played out this cat and mouse game many times, and every time the result would have been different.

"What corporation you working for?" he asked to keep the conversation going. By his mental calculation they had four minutes and thirteen seconds.

Her mouth formed a half smile. "Not working for them."

He nodded at the terrified Shaw who struggled to free his arms. The chair rocked side to side. With sufficient time he'd probably have gotten free but there wasn't time. "Then why?"

Her eyes became hard and her mouth became a grim line. "Personal reasons."

Bump arched an eyebrow. "Really? Tell me."

"Why should I?"

"Well, for one reason in three minutes and forty one seconds we're all going to die or you and I will disappear in a paradox. So I say why not?"

Surprisingly, she smiled. "Sure. Why not?"

A bead of sweat trickled down Bumps shirt collar.

Three minutes and fifteen seconds.

"Dr. Shaw will have three sons. Two become doctors, psychiatrists like himself, while the third becomes a train engineer. These three men marry and each have two children. Of these the records are somewhat murky due to a paradox but our record does show one boy grows up to found a black market munitions company."

"So his ancestor killed your family, right?" interrupted Bump.

She scowled at him. "Don't be ridiculous. Do you want to hear the story or not?"

Two minutes and thirty-one seconds.

"Yeah, sure. Sorry."

"So, as I was saying my father—"

"Your father?" He couldn't help himself.

"Yes," she crossed her arms over her chest. "My father's company was founded as a munitions company selling arms to the highest bidder. The money made is tainted with innocent blood."

"So you want to clear your conscience is that it?"

"No, it's too late for that."

"But your father's company now manufacturers faster than light drives and has helped humanity to travel the stars and open up trade with countless worlds across the galaxy. That's not so bad is it?"

One minute and twenty-five seconds.

"Unless you've seen the future then I would say you're correct."

Bumps heart froze. Travel to the future was illegal and highly dangerous. Tampering with future events could have disastrous consequences for the past.

She smiled.

One minute and one second.

"What has Dr. Shaw got to do with this?"

"As I said he will have three sons."

So that was it. Wipe Dr. Shaw from existence, no children, and no Shaw's, including Arlene, or whatever her name was.

Forty-one seconds.

"You know you'll be gone too, right?" She nodded. Then he realized she wasn't leaving before the implosion.

Thirty-eight seconds.

He fought the urge to ask her what she'd seen in the future but he knew in his gut he didn't want to know. No one should know. What he did know was Arlene was willing to sacrifice herself to save the future.

Twenty-nine seconds.

He paced the room. "I have to know, Arlene."

"My name's Ariel Shaw actually," she said.

Twenty-five seconds.

"Well then, Ariel I have to be sure I'm doing the right thing."

"I know I'm right. I saw it with my own eyes," she said.

Bump gazed into her eyes. Does he trust her? He had to do what was right.

Eighteen seconds.

Bump looked at Dr. Shaw and saw the raw fear in his eyes. He blinked away the sweat trickling into his eyes. Did he deserve to die to save the future? Did anyone?

Eleven seconds.

"How about I take Dr. Shaw back with me?" Bump suggested.

"Is that even possible?"

He shook his head. "No."

Eight seconds.

"Are you going to stop me?" Ariel asked.

"No." In truth he hadn't fully decided.

Three seconds.

With one second to go Bump decided. He triggered the return worm in the program and woke up in the travel chamber.

He breathed a sigh of relief. He was still here. No paradox. As he stepped out of the chamber and headed for the showers since he'd been in the chamber for the past twenty-four hours.

The memory of the last twenty-four hours began to fade as he stood under the spray of the hot shower. By the time he finished it was gone.

All it took was five minutes and the past was gone forever.

Bump looked forward to his next assignment and wondered where and when it would take him.

# DRAGON RISING

Russ Crossley

"Gargoyle this is Dragon. Over." The stealth drone hovering in the night sky high above the streets of Vancouver boosted her COM signal so she could communicate with command. Without the signal boost her ability to contact the on duty controller would be sporadic at best.

"Go ahead, Dragon, this is Gargoyle. Over."

She spoke softly into the mike in her helmet. "Current readings show grid reference 1-5 is deserted. Permission to move to grid reference 1-6."

"Acknowledged. Permission granted. Good hunting, Dragon. Gargoyle out."

Jesse lowered my arm resting her gloved palm on the butt of her silenced nine-millimeter pistol in the holster on her hip. Her mouth was dry, but she ignored her own physical needs. The mission was too important, hydration could wait. The future depended on her successfully discovering the source of the outbreak.

Jesse Splint stole a peek around the corner of the damp, slime-coated brick wall of the dank alley. The rain slicked pavement and the dark, quiet deserted office towers were all she could see through the night vision ocular units in her helmet. She was unable to detect movement, human, animal, or, thankfully the presence of any undead.

Two hours wasn't a lot of time to complete her mission but that was all she'd been given. She had to move fast.

If she failed she might end up dead, or perhaps undead, but hers was after all a high-risk profession. Her breathing was steady and according to the heads up display in her helmet her heart rate and blood pressure were well within the normal range. The helmet also displayed the current time and date. A countdown indicator had been added so she was aware of the looming deadline.

One hour fifty minutes. Time had become her enemy.

To the untrained eye the streets of the central core of Vancouver appeared deserted, but she knew better. Recent intelligence reports stated the undead lurked around every corner, and in every abandoned building. If at all possible she'd stay in the streets and avoid entering any of the buildings. Staying in the open meant less chance of being cornered by a herd of zoms.

Not that she was afraid; danger was her chosen profession, her calling. Something her late father never understood when she reluctantly told him she was joining Special Operations. She knew how he'd react when she dropped out of medical school but it was her life and she wanted to serve humanity in her own way. She graved action not test tubes.

Jesse brought the sensor unit screen on the armband on her left arm to eye level. A red dot on the six by two inch display represented the stealth drone high over the downtown core. It had stopped moving meaning the device had completed its sweep. The readings confirmed what her eyes were telling her. Being dependent on machines was a curse as far as she was concerned. Machines were unreliable. Your buddy next to you was a better safety net than any machine ever built. Too bad she was alone, but since she had insisted on a solo recon any consequences were hers alone.

She'd been dropped behind the security corridor less than half an hour ago and so far hadn't seen any signs of life, or movement of any kind. At the mission intelligence briefing she was told the inner core of the decimated city was crawling with undead. They should be everywhere, yet the evidence so far suggested otherwise. What else had intelligence missed? Her jaw tightened. Had she been discovered?

Jesse moved quickly and quietly as possible down the deserted alley until she came to the junction with the street. Checking the sensor display again she determined grid 1-6 was located half a click west of her current position.

Rain had begun to fall. Traces of the chemical odor in the rainwater made it through the stealth suits filters wrinkling her nose. She'd never enjoyed the smell of unfiltered water thankful she lived under the dome protecting new Seattle. At least in Seattle the water was safe to drink and the food plentiful.

Making sure to stay close to the ivy covered forty story buildings she hurried toward the new grid coordinates. The area she was heading for was at the intersection of Burrard and Hastings Streets. Jagged tears from minor yet frequent earthquakes fractured the worn, sagging asphalt. The once smooth cement sidewalks were split by the roots of untended trees planted decades ago their root systems expanding and destroying man's work. Knots of weeds and wild grasses inhabited the cracks.

Once at the junction of the two main streets she could see the old harbor and the two convention centers. Intelligence suspected one of the two convention centers was the epicenter of the infection.

Evidence extracted from a captured undead—designated zombie-alpha—was tested. In the things cells the science team discovered minute traces of seawater and pigeon excrement. After the death of the human population in Vancouver upwards of ten thousand pigeons settled in and around the convention centers. No one knew why exactly, but the speculation was the birds were flocking to a food source at the site. Again, no one knew why, and while the drones confirmed the sudden increase in bird population, no amount of machine surveillance discovered the reasons for this behavior.

Jesse knew boots-on-the-ground Intel was best when you needed answers to tough questions. She had her own theory about the bird's behavior, but she was reluctant to share her ideas fearing she'd be laughed out of Special Operations Branch. Her theory was that someone was manufacturing zombies from spare body parts. Sure, it was pure speculation and too horrible to contemplate, but she believed her theory had merit. Her current mission would finally confirm her suspicions.

Her degree in advanced paranormal studies at the Special Operations Academy often made her a target for ridicule by the close minded in SOB. Muscle heads, she mused, brute force was all they understood.

Besides she didn't need the brass' spotlights on her. The truth was she hoped and prayed she was wrong — dead wrong.

Moving quickly along the empty street she occasionally ducked into an alley and held her breath straining for any stray sounds registering in the audio sensors in her helmet. But the only noise the sensors detected was the steady patter of rain bouncing off the wet pavement. The streets were dark and quiet.

As she neared the intersection of Burrard and Hastings she made certain to stay close to the buildings and frequently checked the scans. Her heart rate increased as adrenaline flowed more readily. Still no contact. Her nerves grew increasingly on edge. Something was definitely wrong.

She suddenly stopped when a stray sound of clothing or a shoe being dragged over the sidewalk registered in her helmet sensors.

Pressing her back against a wall made of glass she drew in a breath and held it when a figure appeared suddenly from a doorway fifty yards ahead. The way the thing moved, a lumbering, stiff-legged gait, she knew it was a zom. One shot in the forehead with her nine-millimeter and the thing would be down. While she might feel a measure of pity for the poor bastard who used to be human her orders were to avoid contact with the zoms, find the source of the outbreak, and eliminate it.

The stealth suit made her invisible, but zoms were capable of detecting the scent of the living. There was something about the warm blood flowing in human's veins that attracted them.

One hour thirty-five minutes.

Jesse moved backward slowly while keeping her eyes on the zom. It was a male animal. The pale face was half torn away leaving a blackened gash from the hairline to the jaw exposing the rotting flesh beneath. One eye socket was empty and the clothes were nearly gone from the bone-white, almost translucent flesh. Around the mouth were traces of dried blood, which meant the thing had eaten not too long ago. What it had dined on wasn't apparent though Jesse hoped it wasn't human.

As unlikely as that was the zom's had been swarming the guard posts at the parameter of the security corridor over the last few months and may have made a meal of one of the guards. The news net was reluctant to share any news about the corridor. Bad news created unrest, and the government didn't need any more headaches.

It was in fact the sudden increase in attacks after more than a year of relative quiet in the zone that created the need for a recon probe in the first place. It would have been unlikely she'd have ever gotten a shot at searching for the source of the zombie infections without those attacks. The irony hadn't been lost on her when she presented her argument to command authority.

She was shocked when approval came down from on high so quickly. Two days had to be some kind of record for bureaucratic channels.

The zom had turned and was shuffling in her direction. She wondered if she'd been detected. The thing was alone and since the undead can't talk she doubted other creatures would be coming after her.

Ducking into the lobby of a building she drew her gun and waited. I really don't have time for this, she thought. According to the grid map on her display screen her only options were to let the zom go by her or backtrack and go around. This meant there would be no way to get to the street below Hastings without doubling back. And since time was growing short so she'd hide in here and wait for the zom to pass.

After ten minutes had elapsed the zom re-appeared shuffling along the cracked sidewalk outside the window. Jesse took a step deeper into the darkness and held her breath. The thing had taken a few steps when it suddenly stopped and slowly turned to face the window.

Raising its arms in front of it, the zom slammed into the window creating a jagged crack that ran vertical from the base to the top edge of the window. The creature took two steps backward then again lurched forward and slamming hard into the window causing the window to finally shatter. Shards of razor-like glass rained down all around the thing causing deep gashes in its flesh as it lurched through the new opening.

Since the zom was already dead no blood flowed from the new wounds instead a trickle of black sludge oozed from the cuts.

Jesse held up her gun and sighted down the barrel. The silencer muffled the shot as she fired once creating a perfectly round hole in the center of the zom's forehead. Brains and more sludge erupted out the back if its head and it fell on it's back then lay still.

Stepping closer, careful to avoid contact with the sludge, she studied the creature. When it had been alive the poor bastard appeared to have been no more than eighteen years old. She'd done him a favor by killing the thing that had taken over his body. Stepping yet closer to the unmoving creature she peered closely at the head then her eyes travelled over the river of exploded brains spread across the floor. A sensor in the interface on her arm buzzed softly in her earpiece. The sensor had detected something strange.

The sensor had detected a technological device made of gold and silver and high tech plastics somewhere on the zom. She studied the screen as the sensors further dissected the incoming data and presented her a schematic of the device on the screen. Her eyes widened when she recognized the configuration. An artificial intelligence computer chip had been implanted in the thing. Who would implant such sophisticated technology in a zombie? Why and for what purpose?

Holstering her gun, Jesse hurried out through the now empty windowsill and made her way along Hastings Street. Burrard was close, no more than fifty yards now.

Odd, she thought, that now destroyed zom hasn't been constructed from a patchwork bodies. It's a single human corpse. How could Intel be so wrong? A sense of unease rose from deep in her gut. More was happening here than she'd been told.

Following her mission protocols she could abandon the mission, but her own agenda took priority over those protocols. It was the real reason she'd pushed for this recon and why she'd joined Special Ops. Only a Special Ops agent had the latitude to make adjustments to their orders if the circumstances warranted it. As far as she was concerned this new in formation was worth pursuing.

Of course she would have decided to continue regardless. Her father and brother were trapped in the infected zone when, after weeks of fighting, the army cordoned off the city center. Upwards of fifty thousand people had been sacrificed on the altar of the common good. Though she suspected they were dead, or undead, she wouldn't rest until she knew for sure what happened to her brother and father.

Jesse suspected the AI chip in the zom she destroyed allowed the creature to detect her and that it relayed her presence to someone. She had just knocked on the back door and a reception committee would no doubt meet her. The odds of her surviving the mission had just dropped to near zero. But however meager her chances she had to try.

The scar surrounding the implant in her own chest ached reminding her time was running out.

One hour twenty-five minutes remained.

She had to tell command about the AI chip. "Dragon to gargoyle. Over." Static. Then a faint, broken transmission came over her earpiece. "This is gargoyle... again... —ver."

"Dragon to gargoyle. Signal quality is poor." Her lips pursed. She had to warn them. "The zom's have an AI chip implanted in them. Do you copy?" More static.

She strained her hearing. Finally a faint voice cut through the hiss. She thought it might be an acknowledgement but couldn't be sure. The hiss became steady so she terminated the link.

Looking up into the moonless sky she wondered what happened to the drone. Even the stars were missing though they hadn't been seen in the night sky for at least a century given the dirty air. She'd taken extra blood oxygen tablets prior to the mission to counteract any possible effects if the suits filters failed.

Her brow creased. With the loss of communications her orders were to head immediately to the extraction point, but she had to see this mission through to the end. For her the mission had always been a one-way trip anyway.

Jesse hoped her stealth suit would allow her to get past any more zom's she might encounter. Of course, if every zom had an AI implant then she had no chance. She was betting only a few of the things had the implant. Hell of a thing to bet your life on, she thought. But then I chose the life of a Special Ops agent didn't I?

At the intersection she brought up the street grid on the display screen again. The two convention centers were located a block and a half north of her current position.

Laying flat on her belly hidden behind a knee-high marble wall she crawled to the corner and peeked around the cool stone. The buildings along Burrard Street leading to the convention centers were mostly of glass and steel towers, a hotel sign ran up the side of one. On one side of the street stood an art deco building the color of tan sandstone bristled with gargoyle figures up its length until the structure disappeared in the gloom high overhead.

Focusing her attention down farther along Burrard Street with the aid of her night vision she spotted one of the convention centers. Shadowy lurching human shapes shambled near the entrance of what had to be the convention center.

The figures didn't generate a heat signature so they had to be zom's. Guards perhaps? If these things were meant to stop anyone trying to enter then it was likely at least one had an AI chip like the one she'd already put down.

Studying the zoms using the zoom feature on her ocular implants she focused on each one in turn. She cursed the fact she was too far away for the sensors to detect the chip.

Checking them one by one was taking time, time she didn't have. She wondered if there was a way to tell which one had the AI chip without getting closer.

Her heart rate increased when she noticed one of the zom's standing three steps above near the glass entrance doors. Her eyes narrowed. The things weren't going to stop her. It seemed to be in charge. The thing had a deep gash across one cheek, and it's clothing appeared to be in better condition than the others. Other than the wound on the cheek the creature was in much better shape than the average zombie. She decided it had to be the one with the AI chip.

After counting to three she held her breath then leapt to her feet and began to run as fast as she could toward the convention center. Alternating between releasing then holding her breath she ran, her heart pounding in her chest. The horizontal stitches around the implant sent waves of needle-like pain shooting across her abdomen reminding her failure had serious consequences not only for her but also for the future of the human race.

If the zoms caught her she'd put the barrel of her gun in her mouth and pull the trigger. No way was she going to become one of those things. No way.

The slap of her boots on the wet pavement echoed off the surrounding buildings. Good thing zom's weren't good at detecting sound.

Her arms pumped as she ran, her gun gripped tightly in right hand a finger on the trigger. Glancing briefing to her left she saw the other convention center come into to view. Attached to side of the block long building was an open breezeway where cruise ships used to come along side. There weren't any zom's near the second convention center so she knew the one she was running toward was the target. At least something was going right.

The zom's in front of the building entrance didn't seem to

take any notice of her as she approached. They continued to shuffle and shamble about seemingly unfocused. The creatures were a nightmare collection of jagged wounds, rotting flesh and missing appendages and eyes. Their clothing hung in rags off their disintegrating bodies. The smell of rotting flesh leaked through her over taxed suit filters and was so strong now she could taste it. It soured her stomach. Crap, these things stink.

She nimbly dodged the creatures and danced around them making her way up the black marble steps. She had nearly reached the glass doors when the zom's behavior suddenly changed. The zom she suspected contained the AI chip appeared behind her and grabbed her shoulders with both hands and pulled her off her feet. She landed hard on her back. The other zom's now moved up the stairs coming toward her. She stared wide-eyed over her head watching them. How had they known to come to the other zom's aid? She was about to be swarmed. No way was she going to be one of them.

Raising her pistol to her temple she closed her eyes and murmured, "Sorry, daddy." Squeezing the trigger gradually tighter and tighter, she waited for the inevitable when a sudden sharp pain sent her into a dark abyss.

---

JESSE WOKE IN PITCH DARKNESS FEELING LIGHT HEADED. HER mouth was dry and tasted of copper. Her arms ached. When she tried to move she realized her wrists were tied at her sides. The skin of her wrists felt raw and sore as if she'd been struggling against her bonds.

Her mind raced with possibilities. She might have been rescued, but had been bitten by a zom? If so she'd turn soon and become one of them. Her mind was fuzzy. How long was the incubation period again? Shaking her head made sharp pain shoot across her forehead and her scalp. The hair on the back of her head felt damp. Recalling the zombies coming at her she remembered the smell of them, the pale dead flesh, the rotting oozing wounds. She shivered. Undead monsters. She paused.

Someone hit me. Who? She must have blacked out. Now she was here. But where is here?

Her heart was pounding in her ears, her harsh breathing was the only sound. Struggling she realized she was tied to something flat and hard like a board. Where am I? she thought.

The implant! Ignoring the pain she strained her neck and willed her eyes to pierce the all-enveloping darkness. Was her AI helmet still working? Her sank as she realized she wasn't wearing it any more. How long had she been unconscious? Her heart rate increased and her upper lip was damp with sour perspiration. She didn't fear death, but she had to know what happened to her father and brother before she died.

"Hello?" Her voice echoed then slowly faded. Wherever she was it was a large space.

Suddenly subdued lights high in the ceiling came on adding a soft glow to the room allowing her to see her surroundings. Swiveling her head a sense of unease arose in her. As she suspected the room was large, she estimated fifty-foot square. Along one wall stood upright glass booths containing nude male and female bodies. They looked perfect, athletic and youthful, unmarred by any blemish or wound. Blondes, redheads, brunettes of every shade. Even their skin color was normal, it looked as if blood still flowed in the bodies. Yet they weren't breathing at least not that she could tell.

Were these the stitched together zombies Intel had warned her about? If they were then humanity was in serious trouble. These things could pass for fully human. They could infiltrate us then destroy humanity from within. How was any of this possible and who was behind these creatures?

"You're right to be worried," said a very familiar voice. Shifting her head to her right her breath caught in her throat when she saw who had spoken. The voice belonged to her father. Her heart sang. He was alive, but his hazel eyes had an unfamiliar, unsettling look in them.

Her stomach knotted with excitement. "Father! You're alive!"

Stepping closer her father stopped and one corner of his wide mouth curled up slightly. "Hello, Jesse. It's good to see you."

"Are you here to rescue me?" she asked.

Her father chuckled grimly. He stuffed his hands in the pockets of his gray lab coat. "No. I'm afraid not, my dear." He moved to stand beside what she now saw was a surgical bed she was strapped to. "You and I are on opposite sides of this war. Unless you would like to join Marcus and I."

Jesse's eyes narrowed. What was her father talking about? What war? "Join you?"

Her father sighed. "You and I have disagreed on many things. When you joined Special Ops I knew I'd lost you forever. But now you can leave all that behind and join us."

He turned and walked to stand before one of the glass tubes containing a heavily muscled dusky skinned man. Her father stood with his arms now crossed over his chest studying the unmoving figure.

"We're building an army to bring order back to the world. Ever since the infection created the zombie's I've been in search of a cure. I haven't discovered one exactly, but I did discover a way to control the infected. That's when it occurred to me humanity needed a strong leader to take charge in these difficult times. They need a ruler to lead them. After the infection decimates the rest of humanity I will raise them all. Then I will build a paradise that I and I alone control."

He walked back to her and laid a hand on her left arm. "The zombies I raised here are undead, the AI implants I devised control them. They do my bidding. Your brother was infected and he was my first success. He's waiting outside to greet you, but only if you agree to join us."

Jesse realized her father was insane. The man she knew was gone replaced by a power mad despot. He might not be an undead but he might as well be since he was dead inside.

"Where's my helmet?" she said.

Her father's mouth formed a grim line. He went to a table near a large refrigeration unit with glass doors containing glass bottles of liquids with labels she was too far away to read. He returned holding her helmet. The helmet was made from a cloth-like material and once fitted to the wearer looked like a balaclava. "You mean this toy?"

She nodded. "Will you unroll one side so I see the inside?"

He shrugged and rolled the edge of the helmet back so she could see the data display. The helmet was attuned to her brain waves so only she could read the data. Her heart froze. Ten minutes remained.

"Father, what you're doing is wrong. You know it's wrong. You're playing God."

Her father laughed gruffly then his eyes narrowed and his brow wrinkled. "The world is in chaos and I mean to save it."

Jesse shook her head. "No. I can't join you. I'd rather die."

Her father grunted then tossed the helmet on her chest. It landed with the unfurled edge facing her so she could still see the data. The countdown was now at nine minutes thirty seconds.

In less than ten minutes the mini nuke implanted in her chest would explode then everything in a ten block radius would be vaporized by a blast of superheated air. She'd be dead but the mad dream of her father would disappear with the creatures he'd built.

"I'll be back my dear sweet, Jesse," said her father his tone edged with sadness.

"What are you going to do?" she asked.

He shook his head. "Since you refuse to join me you will not be reunited with your brother, and I will inject you with the infection. I'll implant an AI chip in your brain so you can join my army. Your skills as a special operations agent will be very useful." Her father turned away and walked to the refrigeration unit. He opened the door and selected a syringe still in its sealed packet.

While he was distracted Jesse sensed this was her chance. She could give the abort code or send the code, which would activate the nuke early. Not that ten minutes made much difference, but she didn't want to die infected by the zombie virus.

"Gargoyle this is Dragon, over," she whispered. Stealing a quick glance toward the refrigerator she saw her father hadn't heard her. Of course she didn't know for certain if her transmission would get through, but she had to try.

She swallowed hard then she spoke the code words. "Dragon rising." Immediately her chest became warm. Her lips curled in a small smile. Her message had gotten through. Rest in pea...

Her consciousness disappeared in a blinding white inferno. Mission complete.

End of Empire

Russ Crossley

"MAJESTY, THEY ARE AT THE GATES."

Tsar Nicholas the Fifteenth looked away from the laptop screen where he'd been composing a blog entry about recent events. His bloodshot eyes betrayed the fear that had been growing in his belly since the financial collapse two years ago.

His faithful defense minister, Marshall Vladimir Lenin had been at his side since they were together at the Russian military academy when he was a young Tsarevich in training. His father expected, and in fact demanded, he go through the rigorous academy officer training school.

"How long, Vlad?"

Vlad shook his head. Nicky saw the sadness in his eyes. It was a sad day for them all, and most of all for Mother Russia.

"Not more than fifteen minutes my —" His words were cut off by the sound of an explosion in the distance. His forehead wrinkled as if he were in pain. "We're running out of time, sire."

Nicky sighed wearily and nodded. "Ok, my old friend. Is the Tsarina and my son aboard the helicopter?"

"Yes, sire." A muffled explosion followed by a roar of gunfire closer now punctuated his words.

"Thank you. I have one more e-mail to send before the lines are cut. Then I'll head for the roof. You go ahead."

Marshall Lenin opened his mouth to speak but Nicky silenced him with a gesture. The Tsar still ruled and those who still respected the four hundred year old Romanov dynasty would obey his every move. Marshall Lenin was such a man.

Lenin disappeared from the doorway. Nicky heard the slap of his friends leather boots echoing on the marble floor until they gradually receded into the distance then disappeared into silence.

The crackle of the wood in the floor to ceiling stone fireplace in his study was all that remained. For the moment at least the sounds of battle had finally ended.

Nicky turned his attention back to his lap top screen and clicked on the Internet connection. It opened then he clicked on the bookmark list. He scanned the list until he located the name of his e-mail program. He clicked on the name and the password screen appeared.

Once he was in the program he saw he had a list of e-mails from the every major, and some minor, royal heads of state around the planet no doubt promising undying support for Imperial Russia.

Truth was his cousins in Germany, England, France and the Americas were impotent and had been toothless monarchs for decades. They couldn't support anyone never mind Imperial Russia.

In that time the Russian Empire had thrived. Since the victory over Japan in 1904 the empire had steadily expanded its borders and its influence. The defeat of Japan and the occupation of the Asian countries had solidified the Romanov dynasty's future for decades.

His cousins were jealous of his continued unimpeded rule. They had become puppets of their democratic governments that controlled their old empires.

Russia, and by extension he and his family, were targets. His Secret Police had gathered evidence those same democratic governments were behind the food riots that had thrown Russia into turmoil.

Now he had to do something he never thought he would have to do. He had to run in order to survive. He'd never run from anything or anyone in his life.

Today was turning out to be an ocean of new experiences.

Nicky keyed in the e-mail addresses of his American cousin, King George the Tenth, and copied King William the Fifth of England. he began to type the message.

Dear, Georgie and Willie, I am about to abandon the palace in St. Petersburg for the last time. It is with a heavy heart I must take an unspeakable action to preserve my empire.

My actions today will have dire consequences for the future of the Russian throne. Consequently I implore you, my beloved cousins to reassure your respective governments they must use restraint in these difficult times, and not to take sides in this rebellion against order if lives are to be saved.

I know you are wondering what I mean by these words but by the time you receive this message it will become very clear what I have done.

Remember, cousins I love you as brothers and that my actions are to preserve Russian autonomy not to destroy it. Please urge the politicians to react with caution.

I am your humble servant,

Nicolas, Tsar of Imperial Russia

June 15, 2017

Nicky closed the laptop without exiting the program and hung his head with his eyes closed. He let a single sob escape between his dry his lips.

"Still sending e-mails, Nicolas?" said a throaty woman's voice to his left. He opened his eyes and he looked in the direction of the voice.

In the flickering firelight a woman dressed in forest green and slate-gray camouflage battle fatigues stood in the entryway to the room with an AK47 cradled under one arm. Her black eyes were narrow and her misshapen nose was dirty as were her cheeks and her hands.

Maybe it was camouflage, then again maybe it was just dirt. Regardless, she held herself like someone fully prepared to shoot anyone who stood her path. The palace guard was gone. They had either deserted or joined the rebellion, or they were dead.

Two pineapple type hand grenades were clipped to loops on the front of her bulletproof vest. Nicky thought about the pistol he kept in his desk drawer across the room. Only there wouldn't be time to get it never mind shoot it before she cut him down.

Is this how it ends? he thought, killed in my own study by a single rebel?

The absolute ruler of the largest empire the world had ever known is killed in his own home by a peasant, a common thug. Maybe history would call her a freedom fighter who killed a tyrant in defense of the homeland. The irony of the situation did not escape him.

He'd read of stranger things in history texts. But it seemed an odd thing to think about when the history involved you personally.

"Yes, I thought just one more to my adoring fans might be worthwhile." He stood and walked to a cart next to his desk where there were four crystal decanters containing the worlds finest liquors.

"Would you join me in a drink?"

The woman smirked and walked further into the room. Like the warrior she was he watched her eyes shift to the corners where the shadows were deepest. If there were any threats in this room this was from where they would come.

Finally her eyes settled on him once again. A tight smile played across her thin lips. She let the barrel of the AK47 dip toward the floor but he knew she could have it on a target within milliseconds and fired quickly after that.

He selected two crystal sniffers then pulled the lid off the ice bucket. The ice in the bucket on the cart had long ago melted to water so he replaced the lid and selected some fine brandy. He pulled out the stopper and poured two fingers of the amber, smoky liquid in each glass. He replaced the stopper then picked up the two glasses, one in each hand. He turned to face the woman and froze.

She had the automatic rifle leveled at his chest and her eyes were hard. He braced himself for the inevitable bullet that would rip his chest to shreds and slice his heart into pieces.

"Are you going to kill the condemned man before he makes

his last request?" he said. Rivulets of sweat trickled down his back.

The woman frowned and lowered the gun. "No, I guess not." She walked over to him and grabbed one of the glasses from his hand then moved far enough away that he would be unable to reach her in one step.

Checkmate.

Nicky grinned then lifted the glass to his lips and took a sip. He preferred the brandy with ice but it was still very fine brandy. There was a gentle heat from the liquor on his tongue before he swallowed. He cradled the glass in both hands and moved behind the desk then sat in the ergonomic chair.

The woman downed the brandy in one swallow. "Not bad," she said. "You royal types live pretty good."

He nodded and eased back into the chair. He set the glass on the desk in front of him and placed his hands out of sight beneath the desktop. Carefully and slowly he would open the drawer and get the pistol. Then he'd shoot her in the middle of her forehead and splatter her brains across the room.

"Agnessa."

"Pardon?"

"My name," she said. "It's Agnessa."

"Really? Your name means chaste or holy doesn't it?" He swiveled the chair side to side.

Agnessa's wide mouth formed a grim smile and she turned away from him to scan the study. She moved to a small table where he kept a jade statue of a tiger. A spoil of the war with Japan. The Japanese were still some of the best artisans in the world and they often paid tribute to his benevolent rule with objects 'd art.

"You have some nice things," she said.

"Yes, but they belong to the Russian people not me personally."

His words set off something in her because she spun around

and raised the rifle. After pulling the slider on the side of the gun accompanied by a ratcheting sound of metal on metal she aimed the barrel at his head. "I recall a speech where you said you were Russia, as if we the people were nothing." Her tone was tight and edged with bitterness.

Unafraid Nicky smiled. If he was meant to die this day then so be it. But Vlad would be back soon to see what was delaying him. He needed to keep her talking if he was meant to see another sunrise.

The only concern he had was her comrades would show up before Vlad did and then it would be over. The only good news was the Tsarevich was safe in the helicopter. His son would one day take his place as Tsar and the empire would be saved.

Any way you looked at this day the empire would triumph and live on. The longer he stalled this woman the better his and the empires chances were for survival.

The woman lowered the gun to let it hang loose at the side of her leg. Her lips formed a half smile and she moved across the one of the wing chairs in front of the fireplace. Using one hand she spun the chair so that it faced him behind the desk then sat and sighed. She laid the gun across her lap. He could see now the safety was still engaged.

It dawned on him this meant her orders were to keep him alive. His face cooled as the blood drained away. The rebels didn't want him dead just yet.

A trial. A kangaroo court where he'd be paraded before the world and his so-called crimes against humanity would be exposed for all the world to see. Then he'd be executed.

It was the perfect plan. All the appearances of legality, the outward appearance of law and order, the allegations, some true, others exaggerated broadly or within a narrow definition set by his enemies. If there was one thing he had plenty of it was enemies. Absolute power generated jealousy in the hearts of some men, and burned holes in their souls they would do anything to plug, even if it meant tearing him and his family down. Even the destruction of a thousand year old empire meant nothing to such men.

More importantly a trial would mean the end of Imperial Russian. Even his son would be unable to set aside the alleged atrocities of the Tsar. Bogdan Alexis Romanov would never be Tsar.

For the first time in his life, Nicky discovered the true meaning of fear. His mouth tasted metallic, lacking even one molecule of moisture.

He wrapped the fingers of one hand around the glass on the desk in front of him. His hand trembled so he hesitated before lifting the glass of brandy to his lips. He raised the glass quickly to his mouth, took a large swallow then slapped it on the desk once again. A trickle of liquor ran from the left side of his mouth. He wiped it away with the back of one hand.

His eyes flitted to his captor. Her dirty features were split by a sardonic grin. "Scared, huh?" she said.

He blew out his cheeks and thought about her question. She was right. He was scared. For the first time he was really scared. What a strange feeling. He thought for a second or two he might vomit but he held himself in check by taking in a slow breath.

"Yes, Agnessa, I am scared," he said finally.

She frowned and shifted her bottom in the tall backed chair. "Why? I thought you were the brave Tsar who defeated the United Arab Empire, and who stormed Beijing to bring the Chinese communists to the peace table. You tamed a country of a billion people." She shook her head, "Now you're afraid of one woman with a gun." She patted the stock of the AK47 and grinned.

"It's not you," he said averting his eyes to stare at the fire.

"Oh?" she said. "What then?"

"A public trial," he admitted.

"A trial?" She chuckled. "Every despot faces their day in court eventually."

"I'd rather face God's wrath than be humiliated before my people and the world."

He heard the scrape of her boots over the tiles when she stood, followed by a metallic click he knew well. She had disengaged the gun's safety.

He kept his eyes locked on the yellow and orange flames that had begun to die down. Soon all that would remain would be a red warm glow. The fire appeared to be friendly. At least something in this room was friendly.

The air seemed to move as she came toward him. It fascinated him how time seemed to slow down as if this were a movie or television show when something terrible was about to happen.

He heard her footsteps as she came up behind him. This was followed by the jab of the gun's muzzle being pressed into the back of the chair. It was an interesting sensation because he never thought he would feel something stuck into the back of the leather chair.

"I'm going to die now, is that it?" he asked.

"Isn't it what you want?" came the reply her voice a low whisper.

He started when there was a gunshot. It didn't seem that loud and there was no pain.

I'm dead, he thought. My world is over. He closed his eyes as tears blurred his vision and streamed down his cheeks.

"Majesty?" said a familiar voice.

His eyes flew open and he swiveled to look at the entryway. He recognized the shape of General Stalin standing in the shadows left behind by the retreating fire. In his right hand was a pistol, a trail of white smoke drifted from the barrel.

The gun stuck in his back had disappeared. His heart jumped when he heard it clatter to the floor.

Nicky shot a glance over his right shoulder and saw Agnessa's face, her eyes wide with surprise. Her brow wrinkled then relaxed as pain began to drift away from her nerve endings.

"General?" she said in a hoarse whisper. "Why?" She took a step back out of his field of vision so Nicky turned in the chair to face her.

The dying woman locked eyes with him. "I'm sorry," she gasped her voice a whisper just before her eyes closed for the last time and she collapsed to her knees then fell forward landing on her face. The automatic rifle lay on the floor beside her where she'd dropped it. Her body trembled and there was an unearthly rattle as the air emptied from her lungs.

Her heart must have still been beating because a pool of dark blood spread outward from beneath her. Finally her body relaxed and he knew she was dead.

At least she knew no more pain. He stood and stepped around the pooling blood.

"Please stay where you are, Majesty," said the General.

"It's okay, General. I'm fine. I have a helicopter to catch."

"No, Majesty, you do not."

Nicky felt anger rise in this throat. He looked at the general and realized the pistol in his hand was leveled at him now. What was this all about?

"General, where is Marshall Lenin?" He had to get this moronic officer back in line and see his family to safety.

"He's dead, sir." The General's brow furrowed and he glared at Nicky. "And so is your family. Sir."

His family? His wife, his son. Dead? His jaw tightened. "What happened?"

"A shoulder launched missile. Sir." General Stalin moved into the room keeping the pistol trained on him. The waning firelight flickered off the medals on his chest. And there were a lot of them. Nicky didn't know Stalin well, but he knew he was a hero of the Russian Empire.

The general had received every decoration the empire offered for heroism, and sacrifice yet he had survived every war of the past twenty years. Most of Russia's long list of heroes eventually died in battle. Somehow Stalin survived.

Nicky's eyes narrowed and his scowled. "Who fired at the helicopter?"

"The woman is dead. Sir," replied Stalin his eyes free of any emotion.

"You killed her didn't you, General?" Stalin nodded. "You're the leader of the rebellion aren't you, General?" Again Stalin nodded.

"And you are going to shoot me aren't you, General?"

Without responding Stalin fired.

The bullet entered Nicky's chest and pierced his heart. The sudden blow knocked him off his feet. He landed hard on his back and the air rushed from his lungs.

He stared at the thick wooden beams that ran east to west along the ceiling of the study. They looked solid and magnificent.

He blinked.

The immediate pain was more terrible than he imagined but it quickly began to wane as his heart slowed and the blood vessels that supplied life giving blood to his nerves began to sag until the plentiful flow was reduced to a trickle then disappeared all together.

Death wasn't so bad. His son was dead now he was dead. The rebels assassinated much of his family in the past few months. Aunts, uncles, cousins, both immediate and distant, were gone. No doubt, Stalin would ensure all royal blood would be purged from Russia forever.

The empire was truly at an end.

Darkness crept from the edges of his vision. Stalin moved to stand over him. His dark eyes gazed down at him.

"Why?" Nicky managed to gasp.

"To create a new dynasty, naturally," came the reply.

Nicky's lips formed a gentle smile. All hail, Tsar Joseph Stalin the Fir —

Then world of Tsar Nicolas Romanov disappeared into a swirling dark vortex.

# NEIGHBORHOOD WATCH

Russ Crossley

The flickering flame from the oil lamp cast twisted, writhing shadows over the walls of Pete Simpson's recreation room in the basement of his split-level, four-bedroom house. The large room was a real man cave. Even after all this time, the room still smelled of cigar smoke and beer, though we hadn't had either of those luxuries since this all began six weeks ago. We four neighborhood watch members were seated around a seven-player mahogany poker table. The playing surface was covered in a tobacco-colored leather, with integrated chip wells and cup holders. We were waiting for the arrival of the fifth member of our group. Seven armless, matching leather chairs surrounded the table.

Only we weren't here to play poker.

Along the walls of the oblong-shaped room were burnished steel shelves containing trophies and plaques from Pete's days as a high school and state collegiate athlete. Amongst these personal treasures were his sports collectibles signed baseballs, basketballs, and footballs representing every pro team in the state of Washington and in Portland, Oregon, just across the Columbia River.

In a wide gap in the bookshelves was a sixty-inch flat screen television. Facing the large digital TV were two rows of leather recliners, five chairs in each row. The simulated oak flooring stood up to the punishment of Sunday NFL games and final four weekends.

Pete hadn't been a star amongst his athletic peers but he had been pretty good. Too bad for him, others were better. They received the scholarships while Pete became a used car salesman who lived in our middle class neighborhood on the outskirts of Vancouver. He was trapped in suburbia along with the rest of us.

Of course, his collectibles and trophies were worthless now. No one is going to barter for a can of tuna with a collectible anymore, not when cash money, gold, and diamonds have any value. Especially when you and your family will starve to death without food. Food and water meant survival. How ironic it was that we'd wasted our lives striving for now worthless stuff.

"Where's Oscar?" asked Alice, who was seated across from me, her dark eyes narrowed to slits. She was constantly wringing her hands as if washing them. Her short brown hair was oily and she reeked of sour sweat, but then, didn't we all? None of us had had enough water to shower or bathe for weeks now. We'd thought about going to the river, but being outside our barricaded neighborhood was risky and presented serious security issues for us.

My poor friend, Alice, was nervous and becoming increasingly edgy over the past few days. Recent events had brought us all to the edge of our sanity.

The lacquered pine paneling that lined the walls behind the shelves had always bothered me. Who in their right mind would keep this cheap '60s crap on their walls? I rolled my eyes since I knew the answer without asking the question. A Neanderthal like Pete, seated to my right, of course. With his thinning hair and receding hairline and expanding beer gut, he had become the poster boy around the neighborhood for the fading athlete. Now, of course, he was a shriveled man—half his former size, with sunken, grizzled cheeks.

"Got the time?" I asked Conrad, seated across the table from me. He looked at his mechanical watch and his lips formed a grim, humorless line. "He's more than an hour overdue."

I slapped Pete's left shoulder with the back of my hand. "I thought you said he'd be back with the scouting party by now?"

Pete scowled at me, his piercing cobalt eyes angry. "Knock it off, Liz, I'm as worried about them as you are. We all know the risks."

"Yeah," I said, sweeping stray lengths of my scraggly, dirty-blonde hair away from over my eyes with my arm. I hadn't had a decent haircut in weeks and had decided earlier today to shave my head completely as many of the neighborhood women and some men had done, although I loved my long hair. It had taken years to grow it this long.

"But they promised us we had ninety days," said May. "Surely we can last at least that long." May was Chinese-American, with dark, almond-shaped eyes that seemed to look right through you, and high cheekbones. She'd always been thin but now her bare arms looked skeletal in her sleeveless, pink, cotton top.

I gritted my teeth as my guts twisted. May's words tore through me like a knife, but I knew she was right. The voluntary ration system wasn't working. Individual greed had overcome the greater good. We were failing. The truth, I knew, was not greed but survival, a very human instinct in these circumstances. People in the neighborhood had been hoarding supplies for themselves, not sharing as we had all agreed.

At the neighborhood watch meeting convened a week after they arrived and cut off the power, representatives from every house in our subdivision agreed to work for the common good. Now that supplies were becoming scarce, it was becoming obvious not everyone was sharing everything.

If Oscar and his small force of four men and two women didn't return from the latest mission, it was bad news for the neighborhood. Several times, food- and medicine-scrounging missions had disappeared in the past two weeks. These volunteers were sent out heavily armed, with guns collected from the neighborhood residents for a collective armory. Their unexplained disappearance meant conditions outside the barricades we'd set up after the power grid failed were getting worse, or something too terrible to contemplate was happening. Our role as neighborhood leaders may have also broken down. I wished now Oscar hadn't agreed to lead this last mission himself, but he had explained that we as leaders needed to lead and show the people we accepted the same risks as everyone else.

Before he left, he told me privately he'd determine what had happened to the other teams if he could.

If our leadership failed to maintain control, then we'd fall into anarchy, survival of the fittest would surpass all other considerations, and we'd have a crisis on our hands. The thought of quelling an uprising of my friends and neighbors caused me many sleepless nights.

A few of the neighborhood men were former military, or reservists like Pete, who had skills with weapons. Many of these qualified former soldiers were manning the makeshift barricades, composed of trucks and cars that had been abandoned after the fuel supply was gone and various pieces of furniture, surrounding the perimeter of the ten-block radius we were responsible for. So far, our internal communications system had been working.

We'd been using old analog, battery-operated walkie-talkies, but the supply of batteries, as with the food and water, were nearly exhausted.

Our neighborhood consisted of fifty homes originally containing two hundred and twenty-five residents. In the past six weeks, we'd lost thirty-five in total. Fifteen disappeared on supply missions, an equal number of the elderly and the very young were lost to starvation, and suicides made up the balance of our losses. We were down to one hundred ninety warm bodies. Many were physically capable but I wasn't so sure about many of these peoples mental state.

Suddenly we heard footsteps pounding down the stairs from above us and Sue Burns burst into to the room, her breath coming in gasps, her lean arms and bare legs covered in a sheen of sweat. Her tan shorts and white top were sweat stained and greasy. Her green eyes were wild and unfocused by fear.

In her trembling right hand she held a walkie-talkie. In her left was the AR-15 semi-auto rifle I had given her after she completed firearms training two weeks ago.

"Sue," I said in a voice meant to calm her. "Calm down."

Sue nodded but her eyes flitted between the assembled leaders still seated at the table and she was avoiding making eye contact with me. Her breathing steadied but her worn Nikes still shifted side to side. The woman was as jumpy as a cat on summer-heated blacktop.

I stood, then placed my hands on the sides of her narrow shoulders to steady her and stared into her eyes. "What's wrong, Sue?"

She finally looked at me, but her eyes were placid and eerily free of any emotion I could recognize. It was as if she was now at the center of a hurricane. "Uhhhh...there's a group of armed people approaching the north side of the barricades near Elmont Street," she said, her voice a dry hoarse whisper.

My breath caught in my throat. I looked over my shoulder at Pete, who had visibly tensed. "You and the others go ahead and check it out. I'll be along shortly."

Pete's tanned brow wrinkled and his eyes narrowed. He stood and signaled to the others to stand, too, then nodded. He hurried up the stairs with May and Alice close behind. I heard the echo of their footsteps thump up the stairs until there again was silence. Before they left the house, they would arm themselves and then head for the Elmont Street barricade.

I directed my attention to studying Sue's sweaty features. Her shoulders sagged and I knew the adrenaline driving her was ebbing. I gently took the walkie-talkie from her and set it on the poker table. I then slipped my fingers around the barrel of the rifle gripped in her left hand, intending to take it from her as well.

Sue's normally placid, oval-shaped face shifted to anger, her eyes glaring at me. I sensed the strength returning to her lean frame. She pulled the gun away violently, forcing me to reluctantly release the weapon. In her present state, Sue was probably dangerous to herself and others.

This was confirmed when I saw the look in her eyes and knew she had lost touch with reality. For the first time since the beginning of the crisis, it occurred to me that a neighbor might shoot me. "Sue, tell me what's wrong." I spoke in an even tone so as not to spook her.

"I need the gun," she said between gritted teeth. I stepped back and gave her room, raising my hands in surrender.

"Why don't you sit and we'll talk?"

Sue's eyes narrowed and a bead of sweat ran down her sunburned cheek. "You're trying to trick me. You want my gun." She pointed the muzzle at me, her right index finger hovering over the trigger. "I will kill you...anyone...who tries to take my gun." Her voice was low and threatening.

I smiled and sat down, placing my hands, one over the other, on the table and resting my weight on my forearms. "No, of course I won't take your gun. If you recall, I was the one who gave it to you." I kept my tone light.

Sue's features twisted in confusion, anger, and suspicion all at once. I'd succeeded in confusing her. Slowly she lowered the gun and dropped into the chair across from me, the AR-15 hanging loose at her side, the barrel pointed at the floor. She appeared exhausted, the last of her inner resources spent. A sense of relief washed over me.

I walked around the table until I stood beside her slumping body. Her eyelids were heavy with sleep. I carefully reached for the rifle and managed to gingerly release her now loose grip when she suddenly bolted upright, grabbing for the barrel. I pulled hard and wrested it away from her as she managed to stand, her face twisted by inner fury. Waves of intense hatred from Sue washed over me. I knew, if she managed to keep control of the gun, I was dead and then the others would be next. I had to take it from her. I had no choice.

It was as if the world was moving in slow motion. I took two steps backward as I raised the gun until it was level with her midsection. Without thinking, I pulled the trigger twice. Two loud bangs echoed off the walls and Sue's eyes went wide as she stumbled backward, gasping for breath. My nostrils and mouth were suddenly invaded by the smell of burnt gunpowder mingled with the iron scent of blood.

Sue clutched her stomach with both hands. Dark red blood seeped between her fingers. I froze. She looked at me, her eyes wide, the pain behind them making me want to wretch. I couldn't believe I'd shot my friend. God, what have I done?

I lowered the weapon, letting it fall from my grip. It rattled as it struck the floor. "Sue, I'm so sorry."

Sue's mouth hung open as blood started to trickle from the right side of her mouth. She dropped to her knees, then collapsed onto her bottom with a cry of pain. She moaned softly. I knelt beside her and wrapped one arm around her shoulders as she dropped backward. I sat on the floor, cradling her head in my lap. She looked up at me, her watery eyes filled with pain. Her mouth moved but I couldn't make out most of the words except for "Sorry."

Her eyes closed and her head lolled to one side as the air escaped from her lungs for the last time. I hugged her to me and began to cry, salty tears rolling down my cheeks.

"I'm sorry, so sorry, Susie, I didn't...." I was about to say I didn't mean to kill her, but that wasn't true. I'd had to stop her even if it meant killing her. It was like shooting a rabid dog. Sue had gone off the mental cliff and she wouldn't have come back. She could have killed us all.

I eased her off my lap and let her limp body roll on its side in the pool of blood that had formed around her before her heart stopped. I wiped the tears away from my eyes and stood.

A rush of anger formed a knot in my belly. Those bastards were at fault. They forced us to turn on each other. A lot of good people, a lot of Sue's, would still be alive if they hadn't come to our planet. Goddamned aliens.

---

THE CEMENT FLOOR OF THE WAREHOUSE MADE THE INTERIOR of the vast empty building cooler than the humid air outside. I had my eyes closed as I fanned myself with one hand, grateful for the relief from the oppressive summer heat bearing down on the harbor beyond the open bay doors lining both sides of the structure. The warehouse sat at the end of a long pier, jutting out into the bay.

A cry of gulls filled my ears. I opened my eyes to gaze out

the open bay door nearest me and spotted the gray wings of the snow-white birds circling above the overturned and burned-out ships floating untended in the oily water in the bay. Like the water, the air was still; but I could smell the rotting flesh of dead fish and human corpses entombed in those shattered vessels. The stench used to make me gag but I was well past that now—I was getting used to the odors of death. I'd seen too much of it in the past six weeks, more than most soldiers saw in a year on the battlefield. But we were on the frontline of the fight for survival, and one consequence was witnessing things no one should have to.

"Liz," called a man's voice from behind my left shoulder. I shifted on the steel chair to face him—Al Hamburg, in his battle armor, hefting his assault rifle. His curly blond hair stuck out from the edges of a Kevlar helmet and dark sunglasses covered his eyes. His torso, arms, and legs were protected by body armor. He nodded at me when I didn't reply and disappeared from view behind the warehouse wall where he would stand guard until he escorted me back to the neighborhood. We were five miles from the barricades but I knew Al and his team would protect me. They had accompanied me from the barricade, where they'd shown up to escort me to this meeting. Professional soldiers always follow orders, so I wasn't worried.

Al was the commander of an elite Special Forces unit recruited by the Hsu-Zat to act as bodyguards when they visited our planet's surface. The Hsu-Zat had arrived in Earth orbit six weeks ago and immediately used some form of advanced electromagnetic pulse weapon to take out our technology worldwide. The weapon even used our satellites to send the pulse that threw civilization back into the dark ages. I missed my damned cell phone more than I should. I must have been addicted to the thing.

Airliners dropped from the sky, creating massive destruction and loss of life. Military forces so dependent on technology found themselves and their weapons useless. Even the most EMP-hardened technology was ineffective in preventing this alien weapon from taking it out. The world had gone all to hell, and all that stood between anarchy and order was the neighborhood watch.

I know all this because, for some reason, a Hsu-Zat who called himself Robert—he told me his real name would be unpronounceable—decided I would be the spokesperson for my neighborhood. We'd met regularly, once per week, for the past six weeks. I'd never asked why he chose me, and frankly I didn't care.

The odd thing was Robert answered any question I asked him and had since our first meeting. As far as I could tell, everything he told me was accurate. The human tendency to lie to protect personal feelings didn't seem to apply to these aliens. He casually related the death toll numbers caused by their suppression of our technology and by the disruptions in civil order that soon followed.

If he considered my circumstances dire in any way, he hadn't let on. In fact, Robert had been cold but not unkind to me. That's why I'd left my knife behind, the one I had intended to use to slit his throat as retribution for Sue's death. Even if I managed to kill him, one alien's death wouldn't mean much in the scheme of things.

From one of the open bay doors, Robert entered, flanked by two others of his kind. His crimson-colored features were placid, his two mustard-yellow eyes avoiding me as his brown boots slapped the concrete floor. The sound of the three aliens' footsteps echoed off the high walls. Other than their skin color, they were humanoid: two arms, two legs, everything in the same places as us. It had been difficult for me to distinguish one alien from another until I noticed the small scar on the end of Robert's pointed chin. He later told me this was due to a childhood fall without elaborating further.

His dark blue slacks and brown vest covered a frame that looked lean and strong, yet his voice had always been gentle, reminding me of the sound of a stream rushing over a rocky bottom. His arms were bare, as was his hairless head. His ears were relatively human shaped, the curvature at the top slightly elongated. His companions were dressed in identical garb. There must have been a big sale on alien fashions at the Hsu-Zat Wal-Mart.

Robert stopped in front of me. His long arms, hanging loosely at his sides, ended with elongated fingers near his knees. Neither he nor his escorts had even been seen carrying weapons. Ray guns obviously aren't his team's thing.

One of his escorts went to grab another steel chair from ten feet across the warehouse floor. He carried it back, placing it behind Robert, who immediately sat, his eyes finally landing on mine.

"Hello, Elizabeth," he said in his usual monotone.

"Robert," I said with a slight nod of my head.

His eyes crinkled slightly at the corners. "I am saddened to learn of Susan's death."

I don't know how he knew, but Al probably told him before the meeting. I had learned not to trust those Special Forces guys. As far as I was concerned, they were the aliens' pets.

His words seemed genuine. Robert had either won the Hsu-Zat equivalent of the best actor Oscar or he meant what he'd said. I prefer to think it was the latter because he had never before shown any remorse for the deaths they had caused. At our next meeting, I decided, I would reverse my earlier decision. This son of a bitch was dead. I would probably die too, but the satisfaction would be better than a gold card with an unlimited credit limit.

"I am leaving," Robert said next.

"But you just got here," I said sarcastically.

Robert hesitated and his eyes shifted to an open bay door to his right and the ocean beyond. I glanced out the door. The wind had picked up and small swells had formed in the harbor. The cooling breeze brushed my right cheek. I detected the now familiar smells of almonds and orange coming from the aliens as the wind swirled through the warm air of the warehouse.

Robert's yellow eyes finally drifted back to mine. "Please forgive me. I meant we are leaving for home earlier than expected."

May's words echoed in my mind and my heart skipped a beat. "You said we had ninety days then you'd turn the power back on."

Robert nodded. "Yes, I did, but my orders have changed. I must return home immediately." The alien stared at me, his eyes pleading. He was unable to elaborate. I glanced at his companions and saw them standing stiff as soldiers at attention, their eyes focused straight ahead looking into the distance, appearing uninterested in our conversation. But I knew they were very interested and listening to every word.

"Will you at least turn the power back on?"

Robert shook his head. "No, that is beyond our capability."

I pursed my lips as my gut tightened. The bastards told us when they destroyed the grids they would restore them after ninety days. It hadn't made sense at the time, but what choice did we have but to believe them. Obviously they lied. "When are you leaving?"

"Immediately," he said again. He paused and I could tell his next words were very uncomfortable for him. I braced myself for the worst. "There are nuclear power generating facilities all across your world that are going critical without the power grid. These facilities will soon melt down and send clouds of radioactive material into your atmosphere. Unfortunately, this means all life on your planet will be extinguished."

My stomach churned and my emotions threatened to overwhelm me. Fear, anger, love, hate ebbed and flowed through my mind. "Then what was the ninety days all about?"

For the first time since I'd met him, Robert appeared flustered. His features were a darker red, his skin now the color of pomegranate juice. His hands trembled and his eyes sagged, reflecting a very human sadness. "I'm sorry," he said again. "Orders."

I nodded and sighed. He wasn't a bad guy for an alien. "Okay, Robert." I stood and his two companions suddenly stepped between us. I smirked at the three aliens, then turned and walked away.

The ninety days was in realty a countdown. A countdown to doomsday. The Hsu-Zat had known all along what would happen after they shut down everything. Their arrival was an experiment and we were the guinea pigs.

Once the human race was extinct, the aliens would eventually have a green and fertile planet to colonize without interference from the indigenous population. Sure, it would take time for the Earth's ecosystems to regenerate, but the Hsu Zat had all time in the universe. Our time had run out. Maybe Sue was one of the lucky ones.

I was determined to delay our impending doom, at least in my little corner of the world. The neighborhood watch would continue maintaining some semblance of civilization until the end came. We weren't going quietly into the night.

While it was more likely we'd destroy ourselves before the radioactive clouds killed us, the neighborhood watch would forestall the inevitable as long as possible. Our neighborhood would stand alone if need be.

As for me, I was determined to be the leader I was born to be. I wasn't about to give the Hsu Zat our neighborhood without showing them we still had fight left in us. It's what we humans do.

# ABOUT THE AUTHORS

International selling Star Trek author, Russ Crossley, writes science fiction and fantasy, and mystery/suspense as well as their various subgenres.

His latest science fiction satire set in the far future, Revenge of the Lushites, is a sequel to Attack of the Lushites released in 2011. Both titles are available in e-book and trade paperback.

He has sold several short stories that have appeared in anthologies from various publishers including; WMG Publishing, Pocket Books, 53$^{rd}$ Street Publishing, and St. Martins Press.

He is a member of SF Canada and is past president of the Greater Vancouver Chapter of Romance Writers of America. He is also an alumni of the Oregon Coast Professional Fiction Writers Master Class taught by award winning author/editors, Kristine Katherine Rusch and Dean Wesley Smith.

Feel free to contact him on Facebook, Twitter, or his website http://www.russcrossley.com. He loves to hear from readers.

Rita Schulz lives in Gibsons, B.C. with Russ, her husband who is also a fiction writer.

She loves to read and paint in her spare time. She is learning to enjoy golf, and he is learning to enjoy gardening. They are kept company, and on track, by their two dogs and Glenn, their younger son.

She has written for years and is an alumnus of the Oregon Writers Network and the Greater Vancouver Chapter, Romance Writers of America. To find out more about her and her work visit her website at http://www.ritaschulz.com

# OTHER TITLES BY RUSS CROSSLEY
## YOU MAY ENJOY

The Trudy Wilson Mystery Novel Series

Bad Loyalty

Shear Murder

Buzzcut - coming soon


Blaster Squad

#1 Terror on the Moon

#2 Sea of Death

#3 Planet of Doom

#4 Raiders of Cloud City

#5 Rise of the Empire

#6 Galaxy of Evil

# 7 The Empire Strikes (coming soon)


Mercenary Knights – A Blaster Squad Short Story


Other Novels


Attack of the Lushites

Revenge of the Lushites

My Zombie Prince

Antique Virgin

The Fire In Their Hearts

with R.S. Meger (from Champagne Books)

Zomopolis

The Last Serial Killer

Razor and Edge Mysteries

The Kidnapping of Billy Buttons

String of Pearls

Death by Clown

Beggin' For Murder

Ragged Ice

The Grand Central Mystery

A Strange Case of Undead Murder

Jazz Stiletto Mysteries

A Day Without Sunshine

Skullduggery

Instrument of justice (first published in Over My Dead Body online mystery magazine)

The Amanda Dark paranormal mysteries

Hook Island

Grind Manor

Moonrise Diner

A Father's Daughter

Short Stories

Countdown

Shoeless Moe

Round Up At The Burger Bar:

The Story of Trixie Pug, Parts 1, 2, 3, 4, 5, 6, 7, 8, 9

Five Minutes

Blossom Queen, Barbarian

The Secret

The Family Line

A Shattered Man

Betrayed

Replacement Parts

Clubhouse Heroes

Sounds That Angels Make

Muggins Rules – originally published in Fiction River Volume 12, Risk Takers

Anthologies

Tales of Urban Fantasy

Five Tales of Bizarre Detectives

Tales of Mystery and Suspense

Tales of Weird Fantasy

Tales of Twisted Crime

Tales of The Unexpected

Tales From Space

10 by Russ Crossley

Round Up At The Burger Bar: The Story of Trixie Pug,

Parts 1- 5 The Beginning

Worlds of Science Fiction and Fantasy

More Tales of Mystery and Suspense

Justice Served

Love Stories

Ladies of the Jolly Roger with Rita Schulz

The Adventures of Razor and Edge:

Five Tales From The Quirky Detective Team

An Unexpected Journey

On Edge

Thrilling Adventures

Total War

Courageous

Smile

Non-Fiction

The Writers Tools - The Synopsis

ALSO BY RITA SCHULZ

Novels

*Fire In Their Hearts* with Russ Crossley

*Old Bones*

Collections

*Ladies of the Jolly Roger with Russ Crossley*

*Ten Tempting Tales with R.S. Meger*

*The Fantastic Five with R.S. Meger*

*Unique Tales of the Fantastic*

*Tales of the Fantastic*

*Nightmares*

*The Reckoning*

*The Dark Zone*

*Collage*

*Smile*

Short Fiction

*Blarney*

*Flower & Bird*

*Party Central*

*Once Upon a Time*

*The Scarlet Curse*

*Spoken Words*

*The Brownie's Holiday*

*A Little Old Fashioned*

## ALSO AVAILABLE FROM 53RD STREET PUBLISHING

HTTP://WWW.53RDSTREETPUBLISHING.COM

During this scary time of global pandemics and economic uncertainty we thought it a good idea to offer this collection of stories to hopefully brighten your day a little and give you optimism for the future. We truly hope you enjoy these wonderfully funny, fun, and entertaining stories.

In this collection you will read about a young girl who gives chase to a flying saucer only to discover an amazing secret.

In the 42nd century you will meet mercenaries competing in a futuristic jousting tournament with a surprising twist.

Discover the truth behind Santa Claus as he races against evil to save the world of the mythic creatures of legend.

Learn how two confessed murderers didn't commit the crime.

Meet a man who can fix any machine known to man who is approached by the Air Force to fix a flying saucer.

Meet the Pug family who believe he's who the fattest wins in an alternate universe ruled by the fast food companies.

And many more of these riotous adventures await you just waiting to make you smile.